GASCOYNE

ALSO BY STANLEY CRAWFORD

Petroleum Man

GASCOYNE

STANLEY CRAWFORD

THE OVERLOOK PRESS
WOODSTOCK & NEW YORK

First published in paperback in the United States in 2005 by
The Overlook Press, Peter Mayer Publishers, Inc.
Woodstock & New York

WOODSTOCK:
One Overlook Drive
Woodstock, NY 12498
www.overlookpress.com
[for individual orders, bulk and special sales, contact our Woodstock office]

NEW YORK:
141 Wooster Street
New York, NY 10012

Cataloging-in-Publication Data is available from the Library of Congress

Manufactured in the United States of America
ISBN 1-58567-739-6
1 3 5 7 9 8 6 4 2

TO E.

GASCOYNE

*I*T all starts when I give the accelerator pedal a couple of pumps and turn the ignition key and the starter growls and finally the engine turns over and comes to life with noises that aren't as regular as they used to be. The old Nash which is the last big one they made back in '55 is getting a little tired but I'm faithful to the end and won't let the buggy out of my hands until it gets to the point where she just won't go anymore. Just then the phone rings.

"GASCOYNE?" says a voice I can't call familiar.

"Who else?" I say. "Who's this?"

"Never mind. Rufus Roughah has just been shot between the eyes out in his country digs."

"Don't say. Why tell me?"

"Thought you ought to be among—" and then there's a gargling noise and the thing hangs up.

This leaves me in a puzzled state because the number

of people who've got my phone number I can count on my right hand, and if Roughah's dead it doesn't matter who knows it first or last since nobody's going to bother to clear out their tear ducts over that one.

I slip the thing into drive and squeeze my way into the Bastinado Street traffic mess and run it up to thirty-five, which is what everybody is trying to do in spite of the fact they haven't got around to synchronizing the signals yet. But if you try to go slow they start rubbing the chrome off your rear bumper. Then the phone rings again. It's Marge.

"Hi Marge."

"Hello dear. Say, Ralph brought the Dodge back from the garage and gave me a bill for fifty-two dollars and sixteen cents. Somehow dear I get the idea I'm supposed to pay it."

"Well why not?" I ask.

"Oh. Well you see dear in the past when I've had the car repaired there there haven't been any bills because you said some time ago, Take your car over to Ralph's and I'll take care of the bills."

"Well," I say, "I didn't mean all of the time Marge, after all we've got to sort of share expenses every now and then. Sometimes you are very extravagant, you know."

"Now dear please don't tell me that fifty-two dollars and sixteen cents for automobile repairs is an extravagance. The car *had* to be repaired. It wouldn't run otherwise. It just sat there and made whistling noises."

"Now Marge."

"It's true, ask Ralph. Then name me an extravagance I've done lately."

"Well I can't think of one at the moment Marge but I'll think about it and tell you later. Say I just got an interesting piece of news."

"What?" she asks, not very happy.

"Some anonymous guy calls me on the phone and says Roughah's just been shot between the eyes."

"Well that must mean he's dead then. Are they going to make tomorrow a holiday?"

"Don't know."

"You're sure he's dead?"

"No, just what Anonymous told me."

"Why don't you call to make sure?" she asks. "I'd hate to celebrate before it's time."

"Good idea. 'Bye Marge."

I hang up and dial Roughah's number.

"Roughah residence. State your name and—"

"GASCOYNE here. Give me Rufus."

"Moment sir."

I slip into the fast lane on Bastinado to try to catch the next three signals. They're not synchronized yet here either but if you can get through the orange on the first one you can hit green on the second and orange again on the third and it looks like we've got an orange coming up nicely on the first this time.

"GASCOYNE?" says unmistakably Roughah's voice.

"Right. How's things?"

"Cut the crap. What do you want?"

"Seriously," I say, "somebody said you weren't feeling too well."

"So?"

"So, how are you and what are you doing?"

"Gascoyne I give you two seconds to shape up."

"Okay, honest, who's there with you now?"

"Christ!"

So he hangs up and I squeeze through the orange light at about forty-five which means the second light's all mine. Somebody says Rufus's dead and it's pretty clear he isn't, something's fishy is my verdict, and namely that somebody's planned to bump him off but is behind schedule which happens often enough in this world. But they ought to be back on schedule pretty soon, I'm thinking, and it might be very interesting to be around the Roughah place about as soon as I can possibly get there to see exactly what's going on. But of all the luck, somebody's tampered with the timing of the third signal and all I see is a nice display of red lights. I slam on the brakes and because the right front brake grabs on occasions like this I come to a stop that takes up two lanes and after screeching of tires but no crunching of metal. I back up a little and pull the Nash back into its lane and really bang the accelerator down when the light goes green. According to my memory, this procedure may get me down to Mirindaranda Road without stopping for the two lights in between.

All goes well and I hit the two lights at about fifty and

12

catch the green arrow left onto Mirindaranda Road, which runs east out into the sticks and west square into the Roughah estate where it splits into two other boulevards that go around Roughah's and then through a mess of housing tracts and finally downtown. I'm heading straight for Roughah's now and all the signals are synchronized here so I'm all set. The traffic looks reasonable for the hour and then the thing is six lanes wide so it pretty well handles the shopping traffic, being as it is one of those continuous commercial boulevards with drive-in everything for ten miles, open twenty-four hours a day. I give Chester a ring.

"Chester, you didn't give my phone number to anybody lately, did you?"

"No boss, why?"

"Some anonymous guy called and told me Roughah's been murdered."

"That's good news. No, so far as I know he could have got your number through Roughah himself or O'Mallollolly."

"O'Mallollolly's got it?" I ask.

"He wasn't given it, but I think he could get it if he really wanted to."

"Yeah I suppose you're right Chester."

"Say boss Mark wants to know if you're in or out of the real estate thing."

"Put me in for two thirds," I say.

"Right."

"Anything else?"

"No boss, things are pretty quiet today."

"Good. Look Chester, I'm going to take a look around the Roughah place for awhile so don't call me because I might not be in the car."

"Right boss."

I hang up and let up on the gas a little to pull the speedometer needle down to forty-three which is what you've got to run at if you're going to make all the signals, once you get in step. I swing into the middle lane to avoid the left-hand-turn crowd and it's the best place to be when you're cruising like this because you can pull right or left when you run into that character going thirty-nine wondering why he has to stop for every red light when he can see them turning green way up there ahead very regularly. The secret is, if you've got anywhere from one to three green lights ahead of you, and Mirindaranda Road is one of those streets you used to be able to see down the whole length of but not anymore, with one to three green lights then you're in step, but with four ahead you've got to speed up or you'll get slapped by an orange and then a red and have to start all over again.

I run by the two big shopping centers at the west end of Mirindaranda Road and instead of turning right or left when the boulevard breaks up I go straight which lands me on a small street of fur shops and jewelry stores and pet stores. The street ends at the main gate of the Roughah grounds and I slowly swing left while taking a gander up their half-mile driveway and their house which looks like Mt. Vernon filled with air and pumped up a little. No cars parked up there, and so I roll down the side street that runs past their garage–servants' quarters and the doors are open and the Rolls and the Cad and the Avanti are there as usual, red, white, and blue.

Things look damn quiet for a murder to be going on but then it could be a family affair. Still something tells me somebody's there who isn't there usually and I'm dying to know who. Since I can't go up the drive without scaring away the wildlife I wonder about finding that back entrance I've always meant to look into but never have. I turn left and then right again onto Mangoldia Street which angles through housing tracts down to the south end of the Roughah layout and then runs along it. Just then I remember a couple of things I forgot and give Chester a ring.

"Chester I forgot to ask what's up on the government surplus auction, you hear anything?"

"Got it all lined up. Three hundred jeeps, and you won't even see the damn things."

"Great. On the Jennings case I just thought of something. I want him trailed with a camera as I told you and her also."

"Her?" Chester asks.

"Yeah I think this one's worth playing both ends. Fat chickens."

"Okay boss. Color or black and white?"

"Joker. Always use color for bed scenes."

"Right boss."

About then Mangoldia twists right and starts running along the south side of Roughah's, with his woods to the right and run-down fruit groves to the left they're staking out for housing tracts. I slow down and start looking for a place to stash the car and have the luck to find a bull-dozer and one of those earthmovers dumped off the road and in the fruit trees a little. I swing in and stop the car behind them both which doesn't exactly conceal the Nash from the road but gives the impression that we're all one big family.

I slide out and lock the door and wait until a couple of cars go by and then cross the road to the edge of the Roughah woods and peek in but can't see a damn thing. It hits me then that it's a funny game I'm playing— Roughah is in a way a client of mine and it's me who's got to risk my neck to make sure he's being smart with his own interests. Well that's the way life bounces and so I plunge into the woods and hope for the best. In about ten yards I spot the first trip line and crawl under it without setting off the shotgun, and then I have no trouble finding the other two. Now all I have to worry about are the dogs but there at least I've got something of an in since Marge's sister raised one of the German shepherds in the pack. Nothing to stake your life on but every little bit adds up.

I push my way through the foliage in what I hope is a

circular route toward a prong of the woods that goes right up close to Roughah's second-story study, about twenty minutes' hike I calculate allowing for the congested state of greenery. Nothing's been cleared or cleaned out in these woods and I keep tripping over branches and getting pokes in the eye. After a spell the trees give way to a large expanse of big thick bushes I've never seen before and I have no idea what they are and don't really care either, but the damn things are thick and leafy and I can't see any more than five feet in front of me. At least they don't have thorns and they're pretty quiet as bushes go so I can't really complain besides the fact it's taking me forever to go I'm not sure where, given now the poor state of my sense of direction.

All of a sudden I stumble right into a large clearing and about drop over to find Police Commissioner O'Mallollolly's limousine parked square in the middle and Maxie his chauffeur and bodyguard leaning against the front fender, smoking a pipe and looking at the sky. His back's to me and just as he begins to turn around to see what the noise is I duck back into the bushes and make the sound of the Wet-Wing Swamp Grouse. To my alarm, Maxie bends down and picks up a large rock and heaves it square at my part of the bushes and in spite of the great pain in the shoulder he causes I manage a passable Swamp Grouse panic chirrup with accompanying wing noises and whirrings, which I cut short by tossing a couple of pebbles under the bushes to my right. Maxie throws the next rock there and when everything's quiet

17

goes back to the front fender and his pipe. My wound is a large bruise with fortunately no blood flowing.

I'm wondering hard all this time what O'Mallollolly's doing here on Roughah's grounds. I suppose there's a first time for everything and there's no sense expecting the earth to shake, but after all O'Mallollolly's an elected official and something maybe big's up when he starts paying social calls to Roughah whose only secret is how he keeps out of the fed's hands. And Roughah himself said he left town during election time three and a half years ago because he couldn't stand seeing O'Mallollolly's picture plastered all over town. So I'm wondering how long they've been palsy-walsy like this and why and I'm pretty pissed off at being left out of this one. Been getting a little careless, I think, and decide to change all that.

Maxie finishes with his pipe and knocks the ashes out on his hobnail heel and then climbs in behind the wheel, slouching down with his cap over his head. Well this is nice and O'Mallollolly's big long Cadillac is super tempting, so I carefully and noiselessly slip the silencer onto the automatic and zero in on the left rear whitewall at such an angle that it'll go through the tire into the gas tank. It does just that with a nice little *thunk* and Maxie sits up and looks around to the sound of leaking air and gas. As he gets out I slip deeper into the bushes but turn around to watch him crouching and examining the little round hole in the tire. All of a sudden he jumps up with a horrible look on his face and raises his hands and tries to look at all the bushes at once.

I angle my way around in the bushes to where I figure there's a little path leading up to Roughah's palace from the woodsy parking lot. My guess is right and so I go along in the bushes parallel to the path, keeping about four feet away from it and hoping I won't walk into something I won't be able to back out of in a hurry. I go as slow as I possibly can with a minimum of noise picking each bush branch out of the way and stepping on no twigs or excessively dry leaves, not so easy with a bruised shoulder. Then as I go on the mess gets even thicker with the addition of very strong clinging vines which reduce visibility to three feet and make loud rustling noises. I stop awhile and wonder whether it might be smarter to go out and show myself and take to the path, ducking in with signs of danger or life. This I decide is the thing to do in spite of the evident risks so I turn toward the path only to find that I've lost it and have no idea where I am.

I stand there a minute trying to get my bearings but the bushes and vines are so thick I can't even see where the sun is. Whatever I do now is a stab in the dark so I set off in the direction I think I was going in but now making quite a lot of noise. The trouble is my legs and arms and neck get caught in the vines and having nothing to cut myself free with I have to pull which means causing about ten cubic feet of rustling vines and bushes. I have never been in such thick vegetation. The rate I'm going I calculate a half-mile an hour. Still the vegetation seems to get thicker and I get the uncanny sensation that the stuff is actually growing around me. Visibility is now down to the next leaf, which is the one I'm trying to blow out of my face.

Unfortunately I'm not the nature-loving type that really eats this stuff up so I can't say I'm having a good time. Nothing like reinforced concrete to walk on, I always say, vegetables are fine but on a plate only. Aside from a few bird calls and that sort of crap I learned as a Boy Scout, I've been pretty well able to keep my dealings with nature down to a minimum and intend to continue that way. As far as I'm concerned, the guy who invents an insecticide to kill everything living except us humans is really going to make a fortune. Just what I could use now to clear this bush and vine business out of my way.

All of a sudden I find myself stepping on something squirmy so I pull the vines apart so as to be able to see my feet and when a space is clear there's about a foot's worth of fat snake, its head and tail disappearing into the jungle on both sides. It's got one of those nasty diamond patterns on its back and I'm about to blast away at the thing when it occurs to me that it might be best to leave it alone or wait until his head appears. The thing is moving slowly but I can't tell which way, whether its head has gone by or whether it's backing up. I wait and pretty soon the thing starts to get smaller and in a couple of minutes the tail slithers by with the longest set of rattles I've ever seen, about seven inches.

I chew a piece of Wrigley's over that one and then start going again, now without bothering at all about keeping quiet, since I'd just as soon give a little warning to the snakes and whatever else. Then it occurs to me that I might be going in one great big circle and I'm disturbed at not being able to do anything about it. I was never very good at geometry.

Getting through the vines and bushes is like threading ten needles at once and it gets darker and darker because the leaves above are so thick and then suddenly I feel a dampness at my feet and quickly tear away the vines to see what I am standing in, which turns out to be water, about three inches. I think a moment about constructing a small observation tower to see where I am but the bush branches prove too tough to break and I give up that idea and go on. The water gets deeper so at least I know I'm making progress in one direction. Pretty soon it's up to my knees and then my crotch and fortunately for a good while it gets no deeper. It's not very clean water, filled with black bush and vine leaves and a reddish algae which clings to everything it touches. Visibility increases slightly, up to about three feet again. Around now I think the worst must be over.

But I still haven't got any idea of where I am. I thought I knew the Roughah grounds pretty damn well since last year I went over them when Roughah got into a financial bind and sold me an option on the whole place. I guess I missed this part and think that there's going to have to be a lot of clearing and filling in if that time ever comes.

I keep on wading for awhile and all of a sudden the bottom drops out and in I go over the head, mouth full of algae and dead leaves. I grab ahold of a bush trunk and

21

pull myself to the surface. This is a fine fix because the bush trunks are too close together to swim, not to mention the vines, and the water's too deep to walk in. But at least now I'm fairly certain I'm not going in a circle. The only thing to do is pull myself along with my arms and bush trunks which I do, but very slowly. This turns out to be kind of painful since for some reason half the bush trunks are covered with a sticky saplike substance and the other half with a hard rough bark. Perhaps the bushes are divided into males and females, but in any case the going is rough and sticky and the skin of my hands is getting very irritated and threatening to come off, not to speak of the dangers of infection. Still I keep on in what I hope is a straight line.

After awhile the vine growth starts to thicken in a discouraging way, first high up in the bushes and then progressively lower toward the water, finally leaving a clear space above the water of only six inches. This means I'm up to my neck in water because it's out of the question pulling vines out of the way as long as I have to support my body with my hands on the sticky and rough bush trunks. However, horizontal visibility in that six-inch space above the water is greatly increased and I estimate I can see about twenty feet ahead. This is reassuring except that suddenly I can see something moving in the water ahead. What it is I can't see well enough, but whatever it is starts thrashing around and making unfortunately large waves which make further progress impossible. In order to avoid the creature, which is about seven feet long with a wet and matted furry back. I change my course slightly to the right but am forced to stop because the waves are getting too damn high. There is in fact nothing I can do but thrust my head up into the thick network of vines, which turns out to be right into what you might call a lizard run. At least land must be near. This lizard run is a sort of tunnel through the vine network reinforced at the bottom for heavier lizards by dead leaves and lizard shit, and the traffic's quite heavy. For some reason the lizards don't seem to mind my head sticking through the bottom of their road, some of them just go over me and others around.

After awhile the furry-backed creature stops bouncing up and down in the water and I'm able to go on ahead. The vines begin to thin out some and suddenly my feet touch land under water and pretty soon I'm treading on completely dry land, able to dry out some. About now I begin to fear again that perhaps I have gone in a circle because the bushes and vines are exactly like they were on the other side of the water. But I keep on going and suddenly run into a stone wall with a stairway cut into it and so I climb up it and am greatly relieved to find myself at the rear of Roughah's mansion, near the kitchen with nobody looking out any windows at me.

The best place to observe the house is from the tennis shed which is at the tip of the prong of the woods, because from there you can see the whole sweep of the driveway up the hill and the side of the house that's got Roughah's second-story study and most of the down-stairs living room through two plate-glass windows. I've got a key to a little room in the tennis shed that's got a window out on all this view and I slip into there without being observed, I hope. But of course I run around the place quite a lot anyway so chances are somebody who sees me won't really stop to think about it.

I sit down in a chair in front of the window mainly to rest a little from all that exercise which I'm not used to and before I can bat both eyes O'Mallollolly comes charging out the side entrance chewing on the stub of one of his Hong Kong Havanas. Something's shook him up because the red veins of his face are more bulging and prominent than usual and he's giving shifty looks to both sides. He stops and tries to wipe something off his left hand with a monogrammed handkerchief. He looks at his watch and then back at the house. Finally he tears off into the woods I suppose down the path I got separated from.

But before I can chew this around at all, Nadine Roughah, Rufus's wife, steps out the front door in a slinky black evening gown, diamonds dripping everywhere, all told weighing around a pound I'd say. She looks around nervously behind her and up at Roughah's study and then at her watch and down the driveway. Suddenly Roughah's fire-engine-red Rolls whips around the gate and up the gravel driveway which makes a white S-curve against the grass, and it comes to a very disrespectful stop in front of Nadine. The chauffeur Dmitri jumps out and they passionately embrace with Dmitri sticking his hand down the back of her gown, damn low-cut there to begin with. Finally she gets in the back and they drive away.

I figure the show is over for today and am about to get up when all of a sudden Roughah's latest, a blond large-eyed number by the name of Nancy, comes running around from the rear of the house with not even a banana peel on. All I can say it's a bad day for somebody. She's running like the grass's tickling her bare feet but that's about the only sign of emotion I can read on her bouncing face. She goes in the front door and crosses the living room and that's all I see of her.

I figure now the show'll be complete if Roughah himself puts in an appearance, but I spend a long time just sitting and wishing the chair had a cushion on it and I'm about to pull out of there when all at once the window to Roughah's study upstairs swings open and a coil of rope with knots tied in it every yard is thrown out. Something's on fire, I'm thinking, but then a furry leg with big sharp claws is slowly stuck out, followed by another just like it and the furry rear of some creature about the size of a man, a little fatter. By the time the whole thing gets itself hooked onto the rope and starts to descend, which gives me a good view of its greenish fur and pointed head, I come to the conclusion the thing's a giant tree sloth, or rather a man dressed up as a giant tree sloth because it's smoking a filter tip cigarette. Why is one question I'd sure like to know, and what it was doing up in Roughah's study is another.

Down it comes to the ground where it gets its left rear

claw caught in a rosebush and so has to take off its front claws, which go on like gloves, to get its foot out of the rosebush. The foot comes free easy and then it puts its front claws back on and looks up at the rope still hanging from the window. It grabs the rope and pulls at it but of course it won't give since it was secured well enough in the first place to have supported the fake sloth's weight. Then the creature gives the rope a whiplike motion which has the effect of snapping a windowpane above. The sloth runs out of the way of the falling glass and walks around in circles with its hands on its hips and making a humming sound. It goes back to the rope and swings on it awhile but the rope won't come loose, as he ought to know.

Finally it stamps its feet on the ground and walks around to the front door and goes in across the living room and disappears. In a minute it sticks its head out of the window above and disappears again, reappearing in the living room below and coming out the front door around to the rope which it looks up at. It starts pulling at the rope again and at last the rope gives and comes piling down on top of the fake sloth, which knocks the cigarette from its lips into the matted greenish hair of its chest which instantaneously ignites in a burst of orange flames and thick black smoke.

However the fake sloth doesn't seem to notice the fire right away and begins to coil up the rope. Then it stands up straight with a jerk and starts beating its chest, its head twisting around wildly at the same time. I'm wondering whether I ought to run out and turn a hose on the thing when it dashes down the hill toward the swimming pool, pounding its chest madly and leaving a trail of thick black smoke behind.

It jumps into the shallow end of the pool and sinks right to the bottom, turning the water black and green. It stays down under for what seems like a couple of minutes and I start trying to remember all that artificial respiration stuff, but then it struggles to the surface and climbs out of the pool acting like it weighs a ton, which it probably does with all that water stuck inside the fake sloth suit and fur, probably none of it water-repellent. It stands at the edge of the pool draining itself with water pouring out the foot and hand joints and a long zipper joint going down its front, and after awhile it tries to shake itself dry like a wet dog but the long fur is too heavy with water and all it can do is swing slowly back and forth like an old washing machine, and even then it loses its balance and almost falls right back into the water. Then it takes off its hand-claws and puts them on the ground and with its human's hands bunches up the fur on its body and squeezes it and wrings it out, getting rid of a good deal of water that way.

It's still pretty heavy when it starts back up the hill and has to stop every few steps to catch its breath. As it gets closer I can see where the fire burned through the fake sloth skin, and underneath the man is wearing a white T-shirt with *HARVARD* written on it in crimson. It takes about fifteen minutes to get back to the house, where it coils up the rope and slings it over its shoulder. Finally it limps slowly out the way O'Mallollolly went.

I sit there a long time trying to make out the meaning of all this and thoroughly expecting to see some more action, but nothing happens and the place is as quiet as a tomb so I slip out of the shed and walk over to the side of the house to see if the tree sloth dropped anything. All I find is the charred remains of a cigarette butt with enough lettering on it to make it identifiable as a Marlboro, not much but I keep it as a clue or for evidence, as the case may dictate.

The coast seems clear so I head down the direction O'Mallollolly and the animal went, down the lawn a ways to a break in the woods made by a path I always thought went only to the aviaries. I slip through as quiet as I can, gun ready, and pass the aviaries with three thousand birds screaming their heads off and then go on into the woods. I get to the clearing without incident but get a little scare when from a distance I see O'Mallollolly's limousine is still there. However as I get closer I can see nobody's there for one and for another Maxie the chauffeur must have knocked his pipe into the pool of gasoline because there's nothing left of that Cadillac but a black and brown rusty burnt-out hulk. I get close and look around a little— another car's been here to judge from the tracks, and I suppose Maxie called for help on the radio-telephone after I left.

I follow the tracks into the woods and after awhile come out onto Mangoldia Street about a hundred yards down from the bulldozers and my Nash. I cross the road and walk into the fruit grove and then walk through that so as not to be so readily seen, and am I glad to get back to the car and sit down again on something soft. I start her up and shove it in low and wheel around over the dirt and bounce back onto the street in the direction of Mirindaranda Road. Then I dial Chester.

"Hi Chester, what's up?"

"Just got a call from MacGanymede at Police Tower and he says that Roughah *has* been bumped off and that O'Mallollolly is over at the Roughah place now filling out the forms."

"Goddamn. I'll call you back in awhile Chester."

"Right boss."

I slam the accelerator to the floor and bring it up to sixty, about the fastest I can let the old Nash go on Mangoldia. Well, so Roughah's dead, no great loss as everybody will agree, but what I want to know is what's O'Mallollolly doing so big in the picture? Roughah was bound to get it sooner or later because he didn't know the fine art of stepping on people's toes hard without them feeling a thing until it's too late to complain, but I also thought he was smart enough not to tangle with O'Mallollolly. I don't give a damn if O'Mallollolly did it, but I sure do want to know why I've been kept in the dark for so goddamn long. Also I've got to watch that this sort of thing doesn't go to O'Mallollolly's head.

29

Mangoldia twists up toward the front of the Roughah digs and I shoot up the front past the garage, and what do you know if the red Rolls isn't back in the garage, and then turn in the main gate with quite a lot of gravel flying around. I barrel up the half-mile drive and pull the Nash into the parking slot next to another black police limousine, which must be the one O'Mallollolly has come in.

I rev the engine up and shut off the ignition at the peak to keep the detonations down because the temperature needle is pretty far right, and slip out of the car and walk in the front door of the Roughah palace into the enormous living room. O'Mallollolly's down at the far end standing beside the laid-out body which is mostly covered by a large sealskin rug, and Lt. Pestings and Maxie are pocketing souvenirs from the hermaphrodite collection on the mantel over the fireplace. I walk down to the body scene for a closer look and except for his hands and feet Roughah's all covered up and you can see the body's been moved some because there's a bat-shaped bloodstain on the purple rug about two feet from his head. O'Mallollolly's working on a crossword puzzle cut out from yesterday evening's *Herald*.

"Well?" I ask.

"Suicide," he says. "Simple as that."

"Why?"

He looks at the sealskin rug a moment and chews at his cigar and says, "I just want things simple at the moment, GASCOYNE. Any objections?"

"Yeah," I say, "I just might want to know who did it."

"Don't. As they say, it doesn't really matter because it was either you or me." He laughs himself at that one.

"So you're going to put it out that Rufus Roughah, prominent citizen and big crook, just couldn't take it anymore and pulled the trigger?"

"That's right."

"Not going to sell many papers, that one."

"Not my worry," he says. "Hey Pestings, take this thing away and shove it in the trunk of the car."

Lt. Pestings and Maxie come over and bunch up the sealskin around the body and haul it out.

"Okay O'Mallollolly, what are you up to?"

"Nothing, it's simple," he says with a smile I can't quite believe in. "Roughah's dead, nobody liked Roughah, so let's not hurt anybody's feelings with a lot of personal questions."

"That simple, huh?"

"Sure."

We head toward the door and find Roughah's butler Grant standing in the portico with O'Mallollolly's fedora and gold-headed cane. O'Mallollolly leans over to me and says in a loud whisper just as Grant swings the door open, "Psst, maybe the butler did it."

Grant goes suddenly stiff and his eyes grow wide and then he just keels over.

"No," O'Mallollolly says looking down at the body, "suicide's a lot easier for everyone concerned. Except for the autopsy, that pretty well closes the case, doesn't it?"

Without answering that one I bend down and feel

31

Grant's pulse. I guess he hasn't got any, dead of a heart attack, strange indeed.

Maxie's got the police limousine out on the drive and O'Mallollolly climbs in the back and as they drive off I notice they couldn't get all of Roughah in the trunk because one foot's hanging out and the trunk lid's held down with a piece of yellow twine.

I climb in the Nash and try to figure out what the hell O'Mallollolly's trying to pull. Roughah out of the way's going to make things a lot easier for him, but not so much easier that it was worth bumping him himself which rather looks the case at the moment because of all those people in the house before the murder, Police Commissioner O'Mallollolly's the prime suspect, if there's really a big fat motive floating around somewhere. But whatever the reasons, I should have been consulted. O'Mallollolly's playing games, and I don't exactly like it.

I start the engine up and point the Nash down the drive and dial Chester.

"What's up boss?"

"It's murder all right but O'Mallollolly likes the way suicide sounds. I think something stinks, Chester."

"I'll say."

"Well I'm going to wait a bit and see if O'Mallollolly comes up with any other bright ideas."

"Right boss. Say, I called Mark and you're in for two thirds on the real estate deal, just in the nick of time."

"How's that?" I ask.

"He's getting the land today, surveying starts tomorrow, construction in three or four days."

"And does he know when the freeway's coming through?"

"Two months the state'll start buying the right-of-way and Mark's even got the demolition contract all set up in advance so nobody'll ever know what kind of crap the houses are made of."

"Good," I say.

"And boss, Jennings walked right into the bridal suite of the THUNDERBOLT MOTEL without suspecting a thing. We've got beautiful pictures and boy is she a dish."

"Good, and Mrs.?"

"I think maybe she's got bitten before."

"Well keep at it Chester. And are you still working on the soybean oil?"

"I'm afraid we're going to have to dump it in the sea, not much choice."

"That's all right, you know I'm willing to take a loss there."

"Yeah boss. Say, Marty called a few minutes ago and wants to know if you could use seven out-of-state Lincoln Continentals that are on the way into town now."

"What's the story?" I ask.

"Bad pedigrees."

"How much?"

"Half price."

"Offer Marty a third and put them into AIRPORT RENT-A-MOBILE and see Rolf about papers and plates," I say.

Gascoyne

"Okay boss. Last thing, there are some state and fed tax people sniffing around your bank accounts."

"All of them?"

"Mainly the big one in the WESTBINDER BRANCH BANK. The state man is up for sale but I don't know about the fed."

"What's his name?" I ask.

"Robinson."

"Don't touch him, he bites. We'll think of something," I say.

"Right boss."

I hang up and slip onto Mirindaranda Road and take it easy for a change. Then I dial Marge.

"Well," she asks first thing, "*is* he dead?"

"Completely."

"Let's throw a party dear."

"You know I never throw parties Marge."

"Pooper."

"No I just don't have the time, especially now."

"Why now?" she asks. "Dear you just never seem to have the time for anything. You know I haven't seen you for two whole weeks now and then it was just for a few minutes when you came in to get the keys for something, look I'm not trying to be possessive or anything like that, but—"

"Well Marge I'm sorry but this is going to be a long week too, but it's not my fault that Roughah went and got himself bumped off."

34

"It is ⌣o."

"Stop it," I say.

"Didn't he pay you for that sort of thing?"

"Technically. Say Marge I wonder if you could run up to the mountains for me?"

"Love to," she says. "Something I do all the time without thinking, like brushing my teeth. What's two hundred and fifty miles?"

"Hundred and twenty-five."

"One way dear."

"All I want you to do is take a quick look at Roughah's hunting lodge up there, Condor's Crag, just to see what condition the thing's in."

"What for?"

"Because my bet is that Nadine Roughah's going to unload everything and cut out of here fast and consequently there'll be a lot of bargains floating around, and that'll be one of the best ones."

"Why don't you send Chester or one of your other characters?" she asks.

"Chester's already on an eighteen-hour day as it is and I need everybody else in town at the moment."

"Well maybe. When do you want me to go?"

"As soon as you can."

"Now?" she asks.

"Can you?"

"If you're not coming to dinner here tonight."

"The hunting lodge is more important."

As usual she hangs up in a fit of anger, and I can see her walking straight out to the car, shouting to the rafters, good old Marge.

As soon as I hang up the phone rings right back at me.

"Yeah?"

"Hello GASCOYNE, this is Nadine Corell."

"Nadine who?"

"The late Mr. Roughah's widow."

"Of course." I knew it all the time but I just wanted to see how hard she is, which is plenty hard. "Tell me Miss Corell, how did you get my phone number?"

"Your man Chester gave it to me."

"I see. What can I do for you?" I ask.

"I want to see you. Now."

"Where?"

"At the house."

"Five minutes," I say.

"Thank you GASCOYNE."

"Don't mention it."

I turn left at the first signal, luckily catching the left-turn arrow green, and go around a block which is mostly taken up by used cars and swing back onto Mirindaranda Road, heading back toward the Roughah layout. I'm getting a little hungry so I reach over and open the glove compartment and pull out a big Hershey bar with almonds, but the thing's a bit limp from sitting in the heat and it's really hell getting the goo off the paper into my mouth, sticky like flypaper. I get most of it in and wipe the rest off my face with my handkerchief, and then I toss the gooey wrapping paper out the window and it sails along flat a ways behind the car, I can see it through the rear-view, and then lands sticky-side-down right square on the windshield of a Volkswagen right in front of the driver, who immediately piles into his nearest rolling neighbor left, poor bastard.

I go straight where Mirindaranda splits and in a second am back at the Roughah gate driving up the white gravel driveway. I pull up finally under the wisteria arbor and park in front of my nameplate. I slide out of the car and walk right in the front door without knocking and notice that already they've taken Grant the butler's body away. The Widow Roughah is standing about in the middle of the purple carpet that covers about half of the black marble floor.

"You are two minutes late, GASCOYNE."

"Mrs. Corell, I—"

"Corell is my maiden name. Miss Corell will do."

"Miss Corell—"

"GASCOYNE let us get to the point. I want you to find the murderer of my late husband Rufus."

"Why?"

"I have a passion for facts and I don't think our Police Commissioner does."

"The fact is that Rufus's dead, Miss Corell."

"I want to know how, why, et cetera."

I look her square in the eye and say, "I have the impression you're holding something back."

"A woman always holds something back," she says and

37

lets her arm drop and it brushes against her slinky black gown with a nice little hissing sound.

"You're being vague, Miss Corell. What would I get out of it?"

"Seventy-five thousand," she says.

"But he owes me at least that in severance pay."

"I'm afraid you'll never get that, GASCOYNE."

"Oh?"

"The estate is nearly bankrupt."

I look at her emotionless face for a long moment while she pulls a cigarette out of somewhere near the top of her very low-cut gown and lights it with a long kitchen match ignited by a deft flick of a fingernail.

"How," I ask, "can you afford to pay me seventy-five thou when the estate's nearly bankrupt?"

"The identity of the murderer is worth exactly one million dollars to Rufus's heir, GASCOYNE."

I whistle. "I'll do it for a hundred and twenty-five."

"A hundred," she says slowly in a nasty tone.

"Sold."

"But you don't get a damn cent unless you find him."

"Of course. But tell me, how does it work out that you will get a million bucks if I find the murderer?"

"I can't tell you at the moment."

"When can you?"

"In three days."

I give her the GASCOYNE-eye a minute or two and then say, "Perhaps I should leave then."

"Why?" she asks, blinking.

"And come back in three days."

She smiles and exposes her very attractive gums. "Please don't." She looks at me down her cigarette which she's holding in front of her face. "Stay awhile," she says.

"Thanks."

"Well?"

"Well what?" I ask.

"Start staying awhile right now."

"I really can't," I say.

"Why not?"

"Too many things to do."

"Like what?"

"Something different every time."

"Well," she says shifting her weight from one leg to the other and picking at her teeth with her thumbnail, "what exactly is it you do, or how do you spend your time?"

"In a lot of ways. It just sort of passes, the days slip by," I say.

"You're not being very specific, GASCOYNE."

"How?"

"I mean what exactly do you *do?*"

"Well," I say, "the next thing I have to do Miss Corell—"

"You can call me Nadine."

"Nadine is to ask you a few questions."

"Oh?" she says.

"Would you mind if I did ask you a few questions now?"

"Shoot," she says.

"Ah yes. Tell me, did you love your husband?"

"Passionately," she says longingly.

"The thirty years' difference in your ages didn't seem to matter then?"

"Only at night. There are some nights I will never forget. One for example—"

"That's not necessary Miss Corell, I understand, but I do want to know how much money you had when you married Rufus."

She casts her eyes up at the frescoed ceiling and taps an index finger on her finely pointed well-formed chin.

"Three dollars and eighteen cents," she says.

"Well now Miss Corell, tell me where—and if my questions seem to jump around some, please don't worry because in the end we'll reorganize everything—tell me where you went with your chauffeur boyfriend Dmitri and diamonds early this afternoon."

"To the beach." She holds out an arm and turns it around slowly. "See my tan?"

I look at her tan and arm for a long time as she keeps turning it around, and when I've seen that one she holds up the other for a long time before letting it drop. They aren't very tanned.

"And what happened to the diamonds?" I ask.

"I put them in a safe-deposit box."

"Why?"

"Don't you think that was a good idea?" she asks with a surprised look.

"Yes, but I want to know why."

"Well the diamonds belong to me," she says.

"Oh. That's all right then. But I'd like to know now what Nancy, Rufus's mistress, was doing around the place earlier this afternoon."

She smiles and waves a hand at me and looks away and says, "Your guess is as good as mine."

"What's your guess?"

"What's *yours?*"

"I'm asking the questions around here Miss Corell," I say.

"Of course."

"What *is* your guess."

She puffs on her cigarette and says, "My guess is that they were screwing."

"It's these little things that are important," I say, "so please excuse me if I seem to push a little hard."

"Of course. I understand."

"Now, do you know anybody that likes to dress up as a giant tree sloth?"

She taps a thumbnail on her teeth again and lets fall an ash onto the purple carpet. "No, I'd say everybody I know would like to do that at some time or other."

"Nobody in particular?"

"No."

"I see. Well now Miss Corell will you be so kind as to tell me what Police Commissioner O'Mallollolly was doing here early this afternoon."

Her face flushes and her eyes go immobile and she pulls the cigarette from her mouth with a little *putt* noise.

"I . . . I have never met Police Commissioner O'Mallol-lolly. . . ."

I stride over to the huge grand piano and fling back the keyboard cover and pound on the keys randomly for dramatic effect. At the death of the last discordant note I say, "Miss Corell you have been lying."

"I know," she says quietly, going a little limp here and there.

"What *is* the truth then?"

"Please have patience GASCOYNE!"

"Am I or am I not being hired by you?"

"You are—the first part was true. Here!"

She pulls out a stack of hundreds and shoves them into my hands, about three grand, I reckon.

"All right," I say.

"I should prefer to be alone now GASCOYNE."

I head for the door shoving the wad into my pants pocket and I turn to nod goodbye to her and I notice suddenly she has moved away from the place where she was standing, and I can see now that all that time we talked she was standing on the small bat-shaped bloodstain left on the purple carpet by the late Rufus Roughah.

As soon as I hop back in the car and get rolling down the driveway I give Chester a call.

"Chester did you give Nadine Roughah my phone number?"

"No boss."

"How the hell did she get it then?"

"Maybe Roughah wrote it down somewhere and she found it."

"Could be," I say. "Not very important at the moment, but it's a little irritating."

"I understand boss."

"Good. Now the Widow Roughah says the estate's almost bankrupt and if I find the murderer she gets a million bucks minus my ten percent. Figure that one out."

"It makes sense that the estate's almost bankrupt. We hit him pretty hard though I haven't seen the last quarterly financial statement yet."

"What's the last thing we got him on?"

"The Wyoming oil deal. He lost three hundred grand on that one without knowing it," he says.

"Still there must be something else Chester."

"I'll have the files checked boss."

"What about this million bucks?"

"If I had three guesses I'd say insurance three times," he says.

"Good thinking."

"If O'Mallollolly makes it suicide, there's no money in that for Mrs. Roughah so it's worth a lot to her to prove O'Mallollolly wrong."

"I remember vaguely something about an insurance policy but damned if I know what. You remember anything?" I ask.

"Not a thing."

"You've got photostats of every paper in Roughah's study safe?"

"As far as I know boss."

"Nothing there?"

"Not a thing," he says.

"For a million bucks he'd pay quite a premium."

"Yeah and we'd have a record of it. Must be a couple of policies with different companies."

"Well do your homework Chester and take a close look at this bankruptcy thing just to make sure nobody else's stealing the watermelons. Another thing, put a tail on O'Mallollolly—"

"He won't like that."

"I know but he's an elected official and there's no law against following a man, doesn't matter who he is. Also I want the Widow Roughah tailed, Dmitri the chauffeur, Roughah's mistress Nancy, and check all the costume shops in town to see if anybody's returned a giant tree sloth costume with a big hole burned in the chest. If you find out who, tail him too."

"Roger boss."

I hang up just as the signal on Mirindaranda Road turns green and I make a quick left across the intersection before anybody else really gets going but have to stop for a damn pedestrian and so I block up a couple of lanes until the old lady moves it out of the way, then I get the hell out of there. What they ought to do is dig dark little tunnels underground everywhere, just for pedestrians, and let us motorists get back the roads which belong to us. I floor it and run up Mirindaranda Road North which winds through some low hills that are just getting their first apartment buildings and will be completely covered with them in two years, and if the Widow Roughah sells out her forest preserve that'll make the whole area solid from downtown east to Pastiche Mountain National Forest.

I'm heading downtown now and the top of Police Tower slips into view, which has been the tallest building in town since '56, but only by twelve feet. It's time to have a little chat with O'Mallollolly now because I want to see what he's up to which I have the feeling is quite a lot. He was always the type who liked to play games with nasty little surprises in them but simple enough that any idiot could figure out the score before it was too late. But now I feel like he might be trying to go big time and if he is he's sure starting out on the wrong foot. He ought to know where to start by now.

I slip onto Beachshore Avenue and run through an old residential section of downtown dodging unused streetcar tracks which are left over from a couple of years ago when URBANIAN IMPROVEMENT ADVISORY CONSULTANTS advised the city to convert from streetcars to buses. The city did just that and so URBANIAN really cleaned up on the fat commissions for the buses they sold to the city and right now they're managing a pilot slum project for this area since the city's agreed not to enforce the building codes, and already I can see they've stopped repairing broken streetlamps and signs or towing away abandoned cars or cleaning the gutters. All this is red-hot real estate now and URBANIAN's cutting the apartments up into little

45

bitty holes in the wall and the city's doubled the bus service through here because these people can't afford cars with the rents they're paying. But I do wish somebody would get rid of the old streetcar tracks and fill in the potholes because all this brings out a nasty front-end shimmy in the Nash, though maybe it's just age because the thing's over ten years old now and the front-end joints are probably all sloppy.

Beachshore Avenue drops me right behind Police Tower and as I pull in the back alley I think that this Roughah insurance thing rings a bell somewhere in my head but just can't get through at all loud or clear. No insurance company in its right mind would have insured Roughah's life for more than about ten bucks the way he was generally disliked by the people who carry guns in this town, but this is the logical way to look at it and my little ringing bell is telling me there is insurance but not telling me a damn thing else. Bad memory I'm getting in my old age, I think as I swing into the Police Tower parking lot and slip the Nash into the parking slot with my nameplate on it. Also, Rufus was way down deep the sort of ordinary guy who feels very bad if he doesn't have exactly what everybody else does and he knew damn well that anybody who's anybody's got life insurance in this world. With exceptions of course, which he wouldn't have understood.

I ease myself out of the car and walk through the little Japanese garden to the side entrance and slip my key into the executive elevator that stinks to high heaven of O'Mallollolly's phony Havanas. I push fifteen and up I go and I turn on the fan to clean out the stink, filthy habit, and in a moment the door slides open at floor fifteen and the small circular waiting room that's never used. I walk across and into O'Mallollolly's plate-glass office and find him peering through the 75X Ziess refracting telescope that's mounted on the end of his very long desk. He's looking somewhere into the city.

"What do you see?" I ask.

"There's somebody with my wife," he says.

"Who?"

"Don't know. Just beginning to make out the license number. I'll fix his wagon."

He writes down a couple of figures on a piece of paper and pulls himself away from the telescope and then screws a black plastic cover over the eyepiece. That's not so much to protect the lens as to keep others from looking through it. The bastard keeps the thing all to himself.

"Well GASCOYNE," he says, "I'm just wondering if I can guess what brings you on one of your rare visits to Police Tower, let me think. It couldn't be that somebody wants you to find a so-called murderer of the late suicided Rufus Roughah, could it now?"

"Who told you?" I ask.

"And it couldn't be that that somebody who's hired you is pretty little Nadine Roughah, could it now?"

"How do you know?"

"And it couldn't be she's offered a nice round sum for this, could it now?"

"Quit playing games, O'Mallollolly, what are you trying to say?"

"Nothing, I'm just guessing. GASCOYNE, listen to me and take my advice. Look, we're all happy that Roughah's gone now, aren't we? It simplifies the situation so much, especially for you. Now you don't need the money so why don't you just forget about Roughah and we'll go on the way we always have, only as I say it'll be simpler now without Roughah."

"I think I hear you talking pretty damn big all of a sudden, O'Mallollolly."

"Who me?"

"Yes you."

"Oh no, you know me, GASCOYNE, just another faithful obedient public servant."

"Election time coming up you know," I say.

"Sure, how could I forget?"

"Just want to make sure you're not," I say.

"Don't worry, I'll make it no matter what," he says with a nice smile.

"No matter what, you say?"

"The public just eats up my charming personality," he says and then bellows.

"Be careful O'Mallollolly."

"I am. *Very.*"

"And do me a favor and tell me something," I say.

"What?" he says, "shoot."

"What the hell were you doing at Roughah's a little before he was supposed to have shot himself?"

O'Mallollolly turns a little pale and reaches over to push the button and I notice then that his left hand is marked with an even curve of fresh tooth marks. He pushes the button and one of the doors behind swings open and the Goon Squad marches in with their white uniforms and shoes and dark wraparound sunglasses. O'Mallollolly picks up a fresh cigar and nibbles at it and looks at me with a slight smile. Then he says, "Mr. GASCOYNE wishes to leave now, would you please escort him out."

I stand up and say, "Don't try it, O'Mallollolly, you'll ruin your future."

"Do I look like the type who'd try something now?"

Yes, frankly, I think at that moment and then walk with the Goon Squad out the door and through the reception room. I invite all four of them into the executive elevator with me which makes one of them about pee down his leg with excitement. I push the one button and down we go.

"What's going on, Vic?" I ask the squad leader.

"Oh you know how O'Mallollolly is, he gets into this kind of state every now and then GASCOYNE."

"Umm. No more than usual?"

"No," he says, "I think this Roughah thing bothers him."

"Him?"

"Like you never know who's next. But he'll get over it."

"Sure he will," I say. "Look Vic if you ever need anything I don't care what just let me know."

"Sure GASCOYNE."

49

I shake hands with them and get out at the ground floor and leave them inside the executive elevator so they can ride it up and down a little, pretty clearly a treat for them. Well, Vic's a good guy and though I kind of doubt he knows O'Mallollolly well enough I know he's the type who'd give the alarm if anything really serious came his way and that goes for most of Police Tower. Not a damn thing to worry about, I tell myself as I climb in the Nash and start the old buggy up. Just then the phone rings. It's Marge.

"Oh God it's so good to hear your voice again dear," she says.

"You sound disturbed."

"Oh God you don't know what I've just been through!"

"What?"

"I left for the mountains just after you called and I was followed out of town," she says a little out of breath.

"Get the license number?" I ask.

"I gave it to Chester and he thinks it's probably a rented car. Well anyway I got out of the suburbs and was going into the foothills with the road twisting and all and you'll never guess what happened."

"You ran out of gas," I guess.

"No. The front axle and wheels came off."

"No Marge that's impossible."

"Wait let me tell you what happened. I was rounding the long sweeping curve with those wavy dips in it you know and all of a sudden the front end of the car made a huge leap and came down clank on the road with the wheels gone. Well the back wheels ran over the front with a crash and out of the rearview mirror I could see them lying there on the road, and then the car started spinning around digging huge holes in the pavement with sparks flying everywhere and the loudest noises you've ever heard."

"Well?"

"Well of course there were no brakes and the throttle was stuck full on and there was nothing to steer with and a two-piece gasoline truck was coming downhill around the corner with its brakes locked and skidding all over the road like a snake."

"And?"

"Well fortunately the gasoline truck came apart in the middle and half of it went over the cliff on one side and the other into the bank on the other side, and I came to a sudden stop when the car hit another dip and dug its nose into the ground and went over on its roof."

"Yes?"

"Well I unfastened my seatbelt and pushed the door open and no sooner was I standing up and about to powder my nose than I saw another great big truck barreling down on me. I jumped into the ditch just as the truck slammed into the poor old Dodge and blasted it into a hundred flying pieces, and then the truck sideswiped the ditch or something and turned over and threw its load *all over* the highway with the most horrible crash you have ever heard."

"What was on it?" I ask.

"The truck?"

"Yes of course."

"Seven brand-new Lincoln Continentals."

"Holy shit! Hang up Marge and call me right back and hang on till the line's free."

"What?"

"Do it!"

She hangs up and I dial Chester as fast as I can.

"Chester have we bought those seven out-of-state Continentals yet?"

"No boss, not yet."

"Well don't."

I explain briefly and then let Marge back on the line.

"Then what happened?" I ask.

"Well then the tow trucks and police began to arrive and the garage man looked over the wreckage and told me that the front axle and wheels hadn't come off all by themselves but had been *unbolted*."

"Hmm."

"What do you suppose it means?" she asks.

"Well it's pretty clear somebody doesn't want you to look at Condor's Crag."

"Yes."

"Which makes it all the more imperative that you go up and take a look at it," I say.

"Oh. But dear I'm rather tired."

"Well Marge I know but you're halfway there already and you might as well go on. Stay the night in the Wolverine Lodge if you want. Charge it to my account."

"Well . . ."

"That-a-girl Marge, that's the spirit!"

"Why don't you come up for the night dear? It would be so nice."

"I'll try Marge. Say did you ask Chester to send up a car for you?"

"Yes Ralph's on the way with a new Jaguar roadster from the agency."

"A demonstrator I hope," I say.

"Yes, I think so."

"That's all right then. You weren't hurt or anything?"

"Where?" she asks.

"In the accident."

"Oh no. Nice of you to ask though dear."

"Well I've got to get moving Marge, give me a call when anything new comes up."

I hang up and turn right at Seventh Street and head toward the Infracity Expressway on-ramp, checking the gas and oil gauges, everything okay. The Widow Roughah pops into mind and it strikes me that she doesn't really give a damn about who killed Roughah and that what she cares about is just having me prove that Roughah was killed by somebody no matter who, so she'll get the insurance money, even if a murderer can't be found or fabricated. That makes sense in terms of dollars and cents but why O'Mallollolly wants to cover the murder up completely doesn't make any sense at all, and the trouble is he's got the body and probably the murder weapon. This one, I decide, is going to take an awful lot of thinking about.

I hit the Infracity on-ramp and zoom up it with the left directional signal blinking and merge in front of a semi and then pull left three lanes to hit the fast lane where I run it up to eighty and dial Chester.

"Yeah boss," he says.

"We've got a hundred lemons sitting on the used-car lot and you have to go and do something like send a new Jag demonstrator up to Marge, what's got into you Chester?"

"Sorry boss but there's not one of them Ralph would trust over two hundred miles, especially in the mountains."

"Not *one?* All right, but tell Ralph for God's sake to fix a couple of them up, hell of a lot cheaper wrecking them than a new Jag. Also Marge has got to have something to replace the Dodge."

"Ralph says there's a '52 Hudson convertible, good shape, runs nice."

"Okay, run it over to her place, she'll take it."

"Say boss I just got the news that Louis slipped through TJ last night with a twenty-pound load."

"Great," I say. "When's he due in?"

"About seven hours."

"Call me right off when you hear."

"Will do."

I hang up in time to scoot over to the slow lane and catch the Nuvappian Boulevard off-ramp, thinking that Nancy, Roughah's mistress, might be in a talking mood at the moment. I brake and make the green light at the bottom and turn left onto Nuvappian Boulevard, the flashiest street this side of Las Vegas but for all its glitter not very profitable. I drive a couple of blocks and turn right at the ANOTHER ROBERT G. LOVE'S FOOT-LONG HOT DOG STAND onto Rantananta Road where I turn off the ignition a little before Nancy's house and coast to a stop in front of her three-story Greek Revival mansion, damn nice house. A blue Ferrari GT is parked in front and I take down the license number and slip myself out of the Nash and walk across the immaculate lawn to the front door which measures a good five by ten feet and oddly enough has been left ajar.

I squeeze through and am pretty nearly bowled over to find the downstairs a shambles such as I have never ever seen in my whole life. Every stick of furniture and bric-a-brac in the living room has been broken up, torn apart or smashed, the carpet is all ripped up and the padding under that and the floor in places under that, pages from books and other papers are laying and floating around, glassware pulverized, the piano is a heap of splinters and wire and small metal fixtures, the cabinetwork in the walls hardly exists and the wallpaper and plaster moldings in piles here and there on the remains of the floor.

I immediately conclude that whoever has gone through the place must have been damned determined and whatever he was looking for a damned small object. But just then I hear a tremendous crashing-smashing upstairs and conclude he's still here and still searching. I quietly make

my way over to what used to be a sweeping marble staircase but now looks more like a quarry and ease my way
up to the second floor which looks like it's been hit by the
Super Chief—the wallpaper's down, crystal chandeliers in
glassy heaps here and there on the pried-up parquet
floors, a real mess. I'm standing there taking this all in
when there's a bone-banging clang upstairs which drops
about two hundred pounds of plaster off the ceiling right
at my feet. I turn and start up the stairway to the top floor
when I hear the sound of a big diesel coming to a stop
outside, and since the stairway's rather exposed to the
outside I go back down to the second floor and peek
through a hole ripped in a damask curtain.

Outside double-parked is a huge flatbed truck with a
crane on the bed and though the crane is lowered I can
see what is on the end of the cable—a gigantic demolition
ball which I estimate weighs a ton and a half. I look at
this a moment and think and then I see the light. It's
pretty damn clear they're going to demolish the house
and cart away the rubble to sift and examine at their lei-
sure and they've undoubtedly got themselves armed with
all sorts of official-looking papers. And then, crazy things
go on all the time in Betsy Hills so only some crackpot
would call the police.

Of course I'm wondering who's doing the interior dese-
cration upstairs and who's behind him. This is pretty
clearly a professional job and there's no two ways about
it. I'm also wondering what I ought to do. Whatever
they're looking for is probably of considerable interest to

me too, and I calculate that the house was worth at least a hundred and fifty grand before the man with the hammer hit it, and so whatever they're looking for is worth over that figure, simple logic. I'm wondering whether there's any connection with Nadine Roughah's cool million. One thing's at least clear, which is that Nancy, Roughah's mistress, has nothing to do with this because she got absolutely clear title to the house in '62 and nobody in their right mind would tear down a hundred-and-fifty-thousand-dollar house of their own on the chance of making a profit. But somewhere there's a hole in the puzzle.

I do some more addition. There are two guys outside with the crane and another with a dump truck that's just showed up and maybe two upstairs, a total of five, which is too many to take on so I slip back downstairs and out the back door and take cover in some bushes at the end of the rear lawn. Pretty soon the two guys upstairs come down and I gasp when I see one of them is none other than Roughah's chauffeur Dmitri dressed in dusty overalls. They walk around to the front of the house and soon I hear the sound of the big diesel in the crane and decide I'd get a better view of things from the side of the house. I work my way through the bushes and discover a little tree fort that some kid has built in a tree and I climb up into it where I am completely concealed from everybody on the ground. Also I have a damn good view of the front and side of the house.

They start putting the big truck into position and erecting the crane and then another truck arrives with a bulldozer on it and parks across the street. A crowd gathers and two Betsy Hills police cars drive up and the cops get out and start directing traffic, word sure spreads fast. The crane is now fully erected and they test the cables by lifting the ton-and-a-half demolition ball off the ground a few feet and dropping it on the sidewalk which turns to powder, and the tree I'm sitting in shakes.

Then they hoist the demolition ball to a height level with the third story, left corner of the brick and marble façade, and pull the crane back and forth giving the ball a good swing. It strikes the brick wall with a dull thud and breaks through it and goes on through and pretty well guts the roof structure on the way out, and on the swing back it tears down the whole third-floor right wall which makes the roof sag. The second swing shoves the whole damn roof into the backyard where it lands with a big dusty crash and brings down most of the rear wall.

Then with a leisurely figure-eight swing the ball clears off the rest of the third floor including two large bathtubs and about twenty-five interior walls. Next comes the white marble portico with five Greek pillars which the demolisher attacks by swinging the ball so that it goes between the pillars and the front wall which causes the cable to be wrapped around them bolo-style. As the ball swings out and around and back toward the pillars, the cable tightens and one by one the solid marble pillars snap like fresh carrots until they are all pulled together for the climactic moment when the ball comes around a third time and strikes them all together at once, reducing

them in one blow to the consistency of coarse gravel. And
no sooner do they drop to the ground than the cornices
and hand-carved friezes collapse of their own weight and
splatter into pieces on the pile of rubble below.

The bystanders who have grown to a considerable
number applaud with enthusiasm and so do I until I remember that I am to remain concealed. The demolition
ball now goes around the house and gives light taps to the
walls low down near the ground and foundations. Next
the ball is positioned over the center of the house at the
maximum height of the crane. It sits there barely moving
but probably the operator is waiting for it to become absolutely still. After a moment it moves a few inches right
and back which causes it to start swinging some and again
the operator waits for it to stop. I take a look down at the
crowd and read tension all over their faces, it's clear to
everybody that this man's a real artist and is about to try
something really difficult that's never been done before. A
few people close their eyes and put fingers in their ears
not knowing quite what to expect.

Just then the operator leans out of the crane cab and
shouts something at the guy in the truck the crane sits on.
The truck engine starts and I can see the demolisher mo-
tioning the truck driver to back the thing a little closer to
the house. They move about two inches and the demolisher tells him that's enough. Then the demolisher adjusts
the position of the ball to correct for the movement of the
truck and then waits for it to stop swinging. He sticks his
neck out of the cab again and peers up at it apparently

59

dissatisfied with something and finally asks the driver of the truck to get out. Again he waits.

All at once I can see his hand pull the lever and the ball drops into the center of the house out of sight. For the smallest of instants after it has passed through the second floor and the first floor and the basement to strike what I figure is the furnace boiler with muffled booms, everything is so quiet you can hear the next-door canary cheeping and the only thing moving is a little puff of dust just above the hole where the ball went in.

Suddenly and without a sound all four solid brick walls are rent with tiny cracks that grow into fissures and crevasses. The walls buckle and begin to drop to the ground in huge chunks and all of a sudden the second floor collapses onto the first with a breathtaking and very dusty *whomp* and instantly the first floor crashes flat to the ground and lastly the whole shooting match drops into the very deep basement. Not one piece of house stands more than six inches above ground level. Only the thin cable up to the tip of the crane.

The crowd bursts into wild cheers and throngs around the crane operator who gives a sweating hand minus three fingers to his admirers and judging from the shouting and gestures he's turning down offers to wreck houses all over the neighborhood. He's a pretty damn good operator, there's no denying that, but it's also pretty damn clear he was smart enough to take a gander at the floor plan of the house beforehand and spot that furnace and central heating network which gave out the ultrasonic sounds that made the walls fall down in such a tidy way.

In a minute an excavating shovel rumbles over the lawn and starts scooping up the debris and dropping it into a dump truck and when they fill it up another one takes its place, and as I take down the license numbers of them all I find out that there are seven dump trucks. They take the rubble to a place forty-five minutes away, round trip, I calculate.

When they get the basement as clean as they can with the shovel, a crew of twenty workmen goes down and carries the rest out in wheelbarrows while another crew goes around outside and picks up the stuff that's fallen off the house. All this takes a couple of hours, and I can't figure out why they brought the bulldozer since they never use it.

I'm getting damn hungry in the tree house and am glad to see everybody go at last so I can get down. Also the joint's not very spacious and I'm feeling more than a little cramped besides the pain from not sitting on something padded. I turn to climb out and notice a small rusty Pet Milk can in the corner and I reach over to see what's in it when all of a sudden there's a sharp and loud *crack* and the tree house shudders and flips over on its back or roof and plummets to the ground twenty feet below, all of me inside. We hit the ground with an awful racket and the tree house folds up and blows apart under the weight of the very heavy branch which narrowly misses squashing me. I pull myself out of the wreckage with a few curses for the little bastards who built the thing and look around for the Pet Milk can and find it driven into the ground under the branch. I pull it out and stick my fingers inside and take them right back out again when I feel something move. A peek inside reveals a very large and deadly black widow spider which I force out with a stick and then blend into the landscape with a twist of my heel. Back inside the can I find a layer of unidentifiable goo, brownish and bad-smelling, and by stirring my index finger around in it I contact an object a little smoother than you'd expect the bottom of an old tin can to be. Inserting another finger I'm able to retrieve the object which is a shiny gold disk with a small hole punched in it near the edge and the number 95400329 etched in funny large old numbers. The other side is blank.

I conclude that this is what they were looking for in the house. Worth anywhere from a hundred and fifty grand to a million—or more. But how? That's the question to think about.

I stick the gold disk in my pocket and head toward the street and am crossing the lawn when Nancy drives up in her Lancia. She gets out and fumbles for something in her purse and then looks up at where the house used to be and turns around as if to make sure she's at the right address and then at me. Suddenly she rushes up to where the front door used to be and screams, "Where's my house?" Then she turns to me and adds, "All right

GASCOYNE where's my house? What did you do with my house?"

"I didn't do anything with your house. Dmitri tore it down and carted it away."

"The bastard. What did he do a silly thing like that for?" she asks.

"He was searching for something he wanted very badly."

"What?" she demands with her cool blue eyes.

"Beats me." I shrug.

"Well is he going to bring it back?"

"The house?"

"Yes."

"I doubt it. Was it insured for theft?"

"Hell no," she says.

"*Tsk, tsk.*"

"Shut up GASCOYNE."

She hitches up her skirt and sits down on the front stoop exposing a good part of her lower thigh.

"What a silly thing to do," she says. "Never did trust that Dmitri. Just wait till I see him. What do you suppose he was looking for?"

"Do you know if Roughah ever hid anything in the house?"

"He'd never have told me."

"Think Nancy."

"I'm trying."

"Think hard. It's very important."

"I'm trying for God's sake G<small>ASCOYNE</small>."

"You must remember something, some *little* thing."

"Well," she says, "it seems to me now there *was* something."

"Try and remember."

"Yes, yes, of course," she cries, "*I remember now!*"

"What?"

"I remember!"

"Good! What?"

"Yes! Of course!" she says almost shouting.

"Tell me!"

"One day about three years ago," she says, "Roughah came to me here at the house and said, 'Go, I must be alone a couple of hours.' 'Why?' I asked. 'Because I have something to do in that time. None of your business what.' Then he beat me and I left for a couple of hours. I have no idea what he did in that time."

"Is that all?" I ask.

"No. About two weeks ago I happened to remember this and mentioned it to Dmitri."

"And?"

"Dmitri asked me all sorts of questions."

"And?"

"I didn't understand what he was driving at until a little later and then I concluded that Roughah had hidden something here in those couple of hours."

"Which Dmitri also guessed," I add.

"Precisely," she says.

"And so he's torn down the house and carted it away."

"The bastard."

"Well I've got to be going Nancy, see you later," I say.

"What should I do GASCOYNE?" she asks.

"Wait awhile. Be patient. Things will work out."

I squeeze in the car and start her up and make a U-turn to head back the way I came. Then I dial Chester.

"Chester take this number down, memorize it and burn the paper."

I give him the number minus one subtracted from the last digit and also the license numbers I've collected in the last couple of hours.

"What's the first number you gave me boss?" he asks.

"That's what I want you to find out Chester. It may be worth one hell of a lot to somebody, maybe us."

"I'll start work on it right away."

"Good. What have you heard?" I ask.

"First, Gifford tailed O'Mallollolly up to an address on Rantananta Road in Betsy Hills where he mingled with a crowd to watch a house being demolished. He's now driving down the Arthur F. Stravinsky Thruway. Second, Johnny tailed Dmitri to the same address where he started demolishing the house before the rest of the crew got there."

"Where's he now?"

"Out in an industrial suburb called Volts where they've dumped the rubble in an old aircraft factory. He paid over nineteen thousand bucks to UNIVERSAL DESTRUCTION DEMOLISHERS to have the house torn down and carried there."

65

"How'd you find that out?" I ask.

"Oh I thought you knew."

"What?"

"We bought out UNIVERSAL DESTRUCTION DEMOLISHERS three weeks ago because they've got the freeway clearing contract with Mark."

"Damn that's right, bad memory I'm getting. What else's up?"

"Roscoe followed Nancy to the beach where she still is, sunbathing."

"What? Hell she is! I was talking to her two minutes ago. When Roscoe calls next Chester, ring me and switch the call over. I'll fix him."

"Roger boss. Now Nadine Roughah's still at the estate, which takes care of everybody. About this tax man Robinson, it's sure now boss that he's teaming up with the state bank auditors to go through the WESTBINDER BRANCH BANK with a fine-tooth comb and I think we ought to do something about it."

"Hmm," I say. "See what sort of robbery-fire angle you can cook up, Chester."

"Will do boss."

I hang up and the phone rings right back and it's Marge.

"Hello dear," I say, "how are things?"

"Awful," she says.

"Oh? Where are you?"

"At the gas station at the summit of Crankcase Grade."

"What are you doing there?" I ask.

"Well this new car Ralph brought up blew a head basket or gasket or something like that."

"Oh no."

"Oh it's nothing serious. The nice man at the garage told me it would be ready in about seven hours. Oh it's nothing serious. Only seven hours. Just a little wait. What's seven—"

"Calm down Marge, you should be able to borrow a book from someone or something. Don't they have a TV set?"

"No," she says, "I think they don't even have a radio. The telephone's ancient, you know the kind with things on wires you press to various parts of your body."

"Well is there a café around?" I ask.

"No just a bar with four red stools in it. That's where I am now, just having a few drinks for the road. So's the nice cowpoke on the next stool. What's seven hours?"

"Now Marge calm down. Why don't you take a nice walk through the woods and get a little exercise and fresh air, the sort of thing you can't do very well in town?" I say.

"Dear there aren't any woods here. It's ten thousand feet up in the *air*. The trees are all *dead*. That's what happens when you try to exercise up here. You *die*."

"Calm down Marge calm down."

"What do you think I'm having a drink for, to calm down."

"Well you sound a little better already. Call back when you get—"

"Dear I forgot to tell you," she says suddenly.

"What?"

"I'm still being followed."

"Who by?" I ask.

"The same car."

"Well don't worry dear, he probably just wants to see where you're going."

"Gimme another beer."

"What Marge?" I ask.

"I was just asking this nice boy behind the bar for another beer."

"Well all right Marge don't drink too much and call me when you get bored."

I hang up and the phone rings right back, busy day.

"Mr. GASCOYNE?"

It's Roscoe.

"What time is it Roscoe?"

"Beg your pardon sir?"

"I said, what time is it?"

"About twenty after four, I'd say sir."

"Good. You're fired now Roscoe but I'll pay you up to four-thirty. This will give you a little time to plan your trip. Try looking for work up north. I just don't think you'll find a damn thing down here."

I head down Nuvappian Boulevard taking my time and thinking about the little gold disk with the number on it and wondering what the number means. Some sort of key to some door, but good only if you know what door it fits.

Dmitri, I'm thinking, obviously knows more about the gold disk than some people since he went to the trouble to tear down the house, and so the sensible thing to do is go pay a visit to Dmitri.

I turn left at the SOUR GRAPES COCKTAIL LOUNGE and wheel onto the Urban Circle Uptown Turnpike Tollroad on-ramp and get her up to sixty-five by the time I hit the right lane, and all's clear so I whip over to the fast lane and crank it up to eighty-five. A state trooper suddenly sweeps out of nowhere and tails me for awhile all hot and bothered until he catches the license number and backs off.

I look at myself in the rearview mirror and notice I could use a shave so I pull the Schick out of the glove compartment and plug it into the cigarette-lighter socket and shave away, pulling down the sunvisor for the mirror behind it which is a little better for some angles. Mostly though I use my own reflection in the windshield since that way I can see where I'm going. And now as a matter of fact the Tollroad tollgates are coming up damn fast, twenty of them with little signals above each gate, and so I quickly shut off the razor and ring up the central phone and say, "It's me GASCOYNE and I'm coming through number one."

"Roger, GASCOYNE," what's-his-name says.

The signal light above gate one goes green and I turn the razor back on and have a go at my chin as I shoot through the gate at a little less than eighty, then resume

69

speed. Traffic's beginning to get thick at this hour but mostly in the four slow lanes, though from time to time I have to pass some idiot on the right because he thinks he's the only one in this world going over the speed limit. I've got an air horn in the Nash that can be heard ten miles away on a clear windless night but I've got to be careful when I use it because people just sort of shrivel up and die when they hear it and there's no telling what they'll do, some slam on their brakes right there and others run right off the road and some try to open the door and jump out, no telling what.

The Mirindaranda off-ramp pops up and I head for that and give a quick call to Chester.

"Chester do you have any idea where Dmitri and O'Mallollolly are now?"

"Dmitri seems to be on his way back to the Roughah place but we've lost track of O'Mallollolly."

"What? How?"

"I was talking to Gifford a minute ago on the phone and he was about to tell me where he was and something happened and he was cut off."

"Hmm. Wasn't his phone went on the fritz, was it?"

"No, don't think so. He said 'Hey!' in a funny way just before we were cut off."

"Well keep the switchboard open for him, that's all we can do now. Say's the copter been fixed yet?"

"Not yet, tomorrow they say," he says.

"Let's hope."

I hang up and speed up a little to forty-three to get well set in the Mirindaranda Road signal sequence, more important now because traffic's really messy and I have to change lanes about every two seconds just because of the ridiculous number of crazy fools on the road who don't know a fast lane from a slow one and who are so damn anxious to get ahead they'd try to slip in the space between bumper and fender if there were only just a little more room, what a mess. Well if I have to stop for three signals on Mirindaranda Road in a day, then it's really a bad day and I can see it coming up with the next signal, and wham I'm right. I stop but behind a row of imported windup cars and when the signal turns green I'm thinking I would be doing them a real service to give the little red Fiat in front of me for example a real push to get the thing on the move. *BLAH!* you're dead, I'm strongly tempted to go with my big air horn since there's no way to get around the insect, and there are times like this when I think they really do power these things with rabbits and rubber bands and aerosol bombs, they go so damn slow.

So slow in fact that we hit the next signal red and the cars are bumper to bumper and nobody can wiggle out of this one, and so when the light turns green and the little red Fiat inches away from the signal like a constipated snail I think I might as well put it out of its misery. I inch up right behind it as close as I can get, and I can see some secretary is trying to drive the thing, and then I just lean gently on the air horn, *BLAAOUUK!*, and I can see her

71

go stiff and I don't know what she does but I think she must be slamming her feet down on the clutch and gas pedal at the same time because she slows up some and there's a tremendous roar up front and white smoke and then black shoots out of her exhaust and then the roar gets like somebody shaking a can full of marbles and it all ends in a loud crackling—booming and smoke pouring out every end of that little Fiat. The secretary's still hanging on to the steering wheel like she's been glued there and the car's slowly drifting into the lane right so I slip past her on the left side and as I drive by I can see her with her mouth wide open and her eyes rather glassy, her head shaking a little.

I get out of that mess in the nick of time because I can see out the rearview cars piling up right and left and hot damn if I don't make the next signal, enough to make me feel good for the next ten miles.

Pretty soon I get to the Mirindaranda split and go straight and then turn right into the last alley before the Roughah digs, where I park and climb out. I round the corner on foot and come out across from the Roughah garage, doors open and the Rolls and Cad and Avanti still there as usual. I cross the street and go around to the side and climb the wooden stairs to Dmitri's apartment above the garage. A good swift kick springs the door and I step inside and close it behind me. I take a rough survey of the place and think it too well kept for a bachelor. What's more, the toothbrush in the bathroom's never been used and there isn't any toothpaste. Dmitri really lives somewhere else but tries to give the impression he lives here. Why? And where's his other place?

Suddenly I have an uncanny feeling which I mistake for that feeling that at last things are fitting together. Well I'm wrong, because I hear a rustling sound behind me and just as I turn around I get it *clang* right on the head. Then everything goes blackish.

I begin to come to with this sort of nightmare thing where I'm a pedestrian on roller skates trying to cross a twenty- or thirty-lane freeway jammed with cars and the DON'T WALK light blinking on and off, but all that stops when somebody pours water over my head and starts talking.

"What?" I ask. "What?"

"GASCOYNE please excuse me for hitting you over the head, I thought you were Dmitri."

It's Nancy.

"Nancy do me a favor and call my doctor and tell him I'm coming right in to have my head looked at."

I give her the number and she calls. My head hurts like hell and I'm not sure I'm going to live. She must have used a tire iron.

After she calls she helps me down to the car and I talk her into driving me in my car to the doctor's which isn't too far away. We walk around to the alley and I lie down in the back seat and she gets the thing going.

"Go down Mirindaranda Road east," I say. "What did you want to hit Dmitri over the head for?"

"Because he tore down my house, the bastard."

"And tell me Nancy, what were you doing at Roughah's the afternoon he was murdered?"

"Just screwing around," she says. "Hey why do you drive an old wreck like this for?"

"Old wreck? It still runs."

"Oh well you know GASCOYNE. It smells bad."

"Smells all right to me. But never mind, tell me do you know anybody who likes to dress up as a tree sloth?"

"To screw in? I don't go in for that kind of trick," she says. "I like to do it in the raw."

"Umm. Well do you know what O'Mallollolly was doing there the afternoon of the murder?"

She gives a little shriek and swerves and goes through a red light.

"How did you know he was there?" she asks weakly.

"Because I was there too."

She gasps. "I didn't know you were there."

"Nobody else did either. Turn left at Lantana Lane."

"Where's that?"

"Next signal. Well what was O'Mallollolly doing there?"

"GASCOYNE please don't ask, *please!*"

"Why not?"

"There are some things people just must never know," she says.

"I won't tell anybody."

"Promise? Left here?" she asks.

74

"Yes here."

"What's it worth to you GASCOYNE?"

"Third building down."

"The pink one?"

"The pink one," I say. "Look Nancy it never pays to buy information like that. Either you tell me or you don't."

"But I'm broke GASCOYNE."

"Broke? You're *broke?* How can you be when you've been getting exactly thirty-two hundred a month from Roughah for the last three years?"

"How did you know that?" she asks.

"I know most everything. It's my profession. Now you must tell me why you're broke."

She goes quiet and stiff. "I can't. They'll kill me."

"All right we'll talk about it some other time when they won't. Stop here."

She pulls up to the curb and we get out and she gives me back the keys.

"My car's back at Dmitri's," she says.

"So?"

"How do I get back to it?"

"Take a taxi."

"Sure," she says.

I give her a crisp new dollar bill. She isn't grateful. Sometimes she can be a real bitch.

I walk into Doc's reception room which's got the thickest carpet money can buy and soft music piped in everywhere and three large aquariums filled with slow-moving imitation fish, and I give a little wave to the receptionist and then go on in to Doc's office.

"Hey Doc some broad hit me over the head with a tire iron. See what's the matter with it."

"Mmm," he says looking at my head up close.

"And as long as I'm here, expect three girls on Thursday, four on Friday and nine on Saturday."

"Good. Gascoyne, someday you've got to tell me how you infiltrated the Salvation Army Door of Hope. Ha!"

"Easy, ducks in a barrel. Hey, I told you not to eat garlic on the job," I say because boy does he reek.

"Ha!"

"Stop it for God's sake." Disgusting.

"There's nothing wrong with your head."

"You're kidding," I say. "It still hurts."

"Then wear a hat to keep it warm a few days, then take off the hat."

"Quack," I say.

"Ha!"

"Next week," I say, "I want you to raise your rates twenty bucks."

"What do I get out of that?"

"Seven."

"Cheapskate."

"You know where it all goes."

"Sure."

*

I slip out the office and through the reception room and make it to the car. Nancy's gone I see and climb into the Nash and fire her up and then make a U-turn to get me headed back toward Mirindaranda Road. Nancy might crack open, I'm thinking, with a little old-fashion third degree but I've also got the feeling that there's nothing inside and she doesn't know a damn thing. All she knows is that something's going on and why not try to cash in on it, she can't fool me, but if she does have something important in her little head it'll probably leak out in the course of time, no extra charge. With items like her, you've got to be patient.

I dial Chester but the line's busy and then as I'm turning left onto Mirindaranda Road, Marge calls.

"*Hel*-lo dear," she says.

"Hello Marge, how's the time passing?"

"Oh not so bad but I'm horribly tired."

"Tired?" I ask. "What from?"

"Oh nothing dear, just the altitude or something. The air's so thin up here. Like pea soup."

"Pea soup?"

"Isn't that thin?" she asks.

"No, thick."

"Oh."

"Are you all right Marge?"

"Yee-es dear I'm fine, feel great, just a little tired though. My back aches."

"Your back aches?"

77

"Oh I think it's just the bar stool or the altitude or something. So tired. I can hardly hold up the phone. Excuse me! Hee! Oh my legs hurt, I think I've got a charley horse."

"How'd that happen?" I ask.

"Well I must have strained a muscle in my thigh dear."

"But how Marge?"

"Oh I don't know dear, it's the altitude or the bar stool or something. Oh I feel *so* good!"

"I thought you said you were feeling bad."

"Oh no dear, I feel just grr–eat, it's this fresh mountain air that just fills you up and renews you."

"Are you sure you're all right Marge? Are you with someone?"

"No that nice cowpoke left a little while ago. He was feeling rather pooped himself. No there's nobody here but the nice boy behind the bar."

"You're sure you're not drinking too much now Marge."

"No dear I'm just taking a little sip now and then. I even had a cup of coffee a little while ago."

"How nice."

"The cowpoke made it."

"How resourceful of him."

"Not really. He went up to his cabin and made it."

"What cabin?" I ask.

"He has a cosy little cabin right behind the gas station."

"But are there any cows at that altitude?"

"Not a one," she says.

"Then what does he do for a living Marge?"

"Well now dear I didn't ask him. After all that's a very personal question."

"Oh. When will the car be ready?"

"Frankly dear I just haven't got the energy to go out there and ask."

"Well I hope soon," I say.

"Of course dear."

"Well Marge I've got to be going so give me a ring when you feel like talking again."

I hang up and dial Chester again but the line's still busy, very unusual and damn annoying. Suddenly I notice in the rearview a silver Porsche I think I saw behind me earlier on Mirindaranda Road and I wonder whether I'm being followed. My old Nash is no match against anything like that except ballistically, but anything is worth a try. But first I need gas and so I pull into the next BIG DADDY SERV-UR-SELPH STATION and stop the car and hop out and flip open the gas port and unscrew the gas cap. Then I stick the nozzle in and let go with BIG DADDY PURPLE CROWN HIGHER OCTANE ETHYL and tell the boy to shove three quarts of BIG DADDY ROYAL GRADE IMPERIAL 30 SAE SLUDGE BANISHING DETERGENT LUBRICATING LIQUID into the engine and add a little can of Garfield F. Geen's Original Friction Stopper because I've got about seven clackety valves.

About the time I finish with the gas the attendant lets out a yelp and there's steam and water flying all over, the idiot let off the radiator cap too fast which was under great pressure because of the excessively hot manner in which the engine often runs. I close up the gas pump and go up to the front of the car and find the joker didn't really burn himself, a little scared is all, and just to make him feel a little better I have him put in a can of BIG DADDY'S COOL ENHANCING WATER ADDITIVE though I know it doesn't do a damn bit of good.

I remind him he's got to do the glass and tires and I head for the john where I take a leak and a crap and wash my face and comb my hair and brush my teeth with the brand-new toothbrush I lifted from Dmitri's. I always carry a small tube of toothpaste around in my pocket but a toothbrush I can never keep ahold of.

I go back outside and notice that the Porsche is getting a similar treatment at the Standard Station down the street, which means pretty clearly I'm being followed by them.

The guy hands me my bill for fifteen dollars and eighty-nine cents along with thirty-two BIG DADDY PURPLE PAISLEY STAMPS which can be redeemed at the end of every year for the appropriate number of cases of BIG DADDY SUPER KRAZY KOLA which cannot be otherwise obtained or bought from any source whatever. I pull out my BIG DADDY BIG CHARGE CARD and present it to the attendant and he goes through the usual facial gymnastics upon looking at it and of course when he goes into the office I can see him rounding up the rest of the staff to come take a peek at the BIG DADDY HIMSELF IN PERSON. When he comes back I have only one criticism to offer him on how the place is run, which is, "Son, I think you'll inspire more customer loyalty and make people feel at home here if you do *not* erase what they write above the toilets."

He mumbles some apology and helps me into the car which I start with a cloud of black smoke, which somehow happens every time I stop for gas. I bounce out of the station and immediately the Porsche is on my tail out of the Standard Station, I don't know what they've got that I haven't at slightly higher prices, and stays there so close that playing the signals game is out of the question. The only thing to do is to get out of town a ways and then try to clear matters up. I slip over into the fast lane and set the thing at forty-three. Then Chester calls.

"Where've you been?" I ask right off.

"Sorry boss, everything was going on at once and the switchboard just couldn't handle it all so I had to use the private line. Here's the situation. First, the U.A.R. man who was to take the jeeps off our hands didn't show up for the rendezvous."

"Damn!"

"Well we're still waiting."

"Didn't we get a deposit from him?"

"Ten percent," he says.

"That helps."

"Well it's not hopeless yet. Now about this tax man Robinson, he's going into the WESTBINDER BRANCH BANK the day after tomorrow with the state auditor so we've got till tomorrow at the latest to do something boss. Flash Fingers is willing to heist and fire the bank tonight even,

81

for forty grand of clean money, for example an immediate deposit in a Manhattan account of his. He'll give back to us whatever he takes tonight whatever way you want, the sooner the better for him. I told him about the tunnel you've had dug to the vault, and he thinks a good hot fire'll be an easy proposition. He suggests he leave a bunch of shell cartridges lying around for the heat to set off."

"Oh?"

"Yeah boss, with all those shells going off the fire department will be scared to go inside."

"Of course, I see. Well tell him he can do it for thirty grand," I say.

"All right, he'll take that boss. Now the next thing is insurance. We were going through some of Roughah's office records for a couple of years ago and we found a vague reference to an insurance policy, that is, something about the high price of premiums."

"That sure rings a bell somewhere Chester."

"Wish I could help you boss but the thing dates from before my time."

"Well keep looking."

"Will do—" he says but is cut short by a coughing spasm like I've never heard before.

"What's the matter, you don't sound so well Chester."

"Just a little tired boss."

"Well hang on for another week Chester and I'll let you have a little vacation. Just can't spare you now, you know that."

"Boss I wouldn't think of asking for a vacation until we get this Roughah thing settled."

"That's the spirit Chester."

The Porsche is still on my tail when I hang up, and Mirindaranda Road is thinning out some but not enough to do anything much about it so I turn right on Mallarmee Village Road and slam the accelerator to the floor, making the old Nash really shudder and howl at the tires a second. Mallarmee cuts through a third-rate commercial center of lumber yards and hardware stores and war-surplus joints whose profits might look interesting to a small boy with a couple of dogs to feed but not me, and then it hits Wrecking Row, the largest string of junk and wrecking yards I've ever seen anywhere, running at about five miles long. I get the Nash up to sixty, a little over the limit, and cruise down the fast lane taking a gander here and there to see if there's anything interesting been towed into the yards. A good place to pick up a car, in fact I got the old Nash down here way back when—it had been stripped of chrome and paint and glass from a sand storm—for almost nothing because it's pretty clear it's in these guys' interest to tell the poor average motorist and his insurance company that his car will never run again in a straight line or the doors'll never stay closed. And on the other hand the market for this sort of goods isn't the best so things are cheap if you know what you're getting, and this is where most of the new used cars, as we call them, from Ralph's lot come. Old Ralph sends somebody by every day to see

the latest crop and to pick the best to take back and make
as good as new again if that's possible. He won't touch
anything but this year's or last's models so we do pretty
well.

I roll past piles and heaps and rows of cars that have
had it in one way or another and wish I could stop and
poke through a couple of yards because that's one of the
things I like to do best to pass the time, especially in a
junk yard that's got cars running back into the thirties and
miscellaneous mechanical junk besides. There's something
about stumbling across an old maroon '47 Ford sedan, for
example, that's been totaled on the front end in a nasty
way, that's really moving because it calls back those days,
not so far away really, with the new Fords in the show-
rooms and the smell and glitter and the ads all over,
"There's a Ford in YOUR Future," and you can see all this
in a rusty wreck with the steering wheel smashed up into
the windshield, and that's the amazing thing. Of course
it's a little sad in a way that new cars get old and rusty
but that's what keeps the economy moving.

I get a bit of a laugh when I run past one place and
catch a glimpse of what looks like the charred remains of
O'Mallollolly's Cad limousine and think that's one that
might be picked up for a song, looks like the engine hasn't
been touched. Two months old, as I recall. A little paint
and upholstery and it'll look like new.

The rearview tells me the Porsche is still on my tail so I
swing left onto State Highway 7 and head toward the
Mallarmee Badlands. The road quickly narrows down to

two lanes and hits farming country without too much traffic for the hour. Now's the time to shake them I think, so I floor the thing and run it up to ninety, the fastest it'll go, and turn on the headlights and the flashing red light and the siren and lean on the air horn while pulling into the left-hand lane. This clears the highway nicely but the trouble is the Porsche can also go ninety and probably more and so it's sitting on my tail having a nice ride as I clear the way, really annoying.

The farmland whips by pretty fast at least and soon we hit the hills and gulleys and canyons of Mallarmee Badlands and I have to pull back into the right lane and slow down because of the blind corners. I handle them pretty well in spite of the tires screaming their heads off and the right side of the car shuddering something awful on all the curves left, but then I begin to notice a slow drop in oil pressure and a slow rise in engine temperature and I begin to worry a little and it's pretty clear this is one race I'm not going to win.

Then with one hand whipping the steering wheel through the curves I pull out my automatic with the other and unscrew the safety just as I hit a very sharp curve. The right front end of the car starts going *whackety-whack-whomp* with a lot of bouncing up and down and then the front tire goes out with a boom and I finish the curve in a nice four-wheel drift backwards, which deposits me otherwise unharmed on a nice wide hard shoulder. I turn off the ignition and crouch down behind the door as best I can, gun ready.

In a second the Porsche buzzes around the corner in a sloppy rear-end drift, rubber flying, then slams on its brakes and slides screaming past me. There's a crunch of gears and the thing backs up and pulls even with my door and I hold my fire because I can see pretty clearly I'm outnumbered by five very large men jammed into that sardine can.

"Having trouble?" asks the driver, who's got a green felt hat on with a feather in it.

"No just stopped to let the tire take a leak."

The guy with the feather slams his gloved hands against the steering wheel and cackles a moment and turns to the guy next to him and mumbles something. Then everybody in the car cackles and slams their gloved hands against things, making quite a racket which must be pretty unbearable inside that can.

"Let us help you change it," the feather says.

"Wouldn't think of it."

"Oh please," he says as if he's carrying a big bowl and God knows what in his gloved hands, "we have not anything else to do."

About then I think I detect a slight foreign accent, sounds German.

"But you will get your gloves dirty," I say.

"We have others."

I smell something fishy but it's pretty hard talking fast when you've got a flat tire underneath you and wondering what they're carrying all those gloves around for.

"We even have a pair for you," he adds.

About then I really begin to smell a rat and the thought hits me pretty hard and clear that you wear gloves to do a dirty job so you don't get your hands dirty and *that job wasn't changing my tire.*

"What size?" I ask to stall a little.

"All sizes," he says.

The Porsche's exhaust goes *punk-punk-punk-ta-punk* and I try to think of a fast way out of this one.

"You O'Mallollolly's boys?" I ask.

Feather looks at me kind of funny and scratches his chin and mumbles something to Glovesies next to him. Glovesies shrugs.

"Never heard of him," Feather says to me which pretty well throws me off my saddle.

"Okay you guys just what *do* you want?" I ask.

"To change your tire," says Feather.

"No thanks, I'll do it myself," I say as menacingly as I can, which isn't tame.

"As you wish," says Feather with a shrug and then he throws the tin can into gear and just then I remember I haven't got a wheel wrench.

"Hey wait a minute!" I yell.

He stops the car and backs up.

"Say do you suppose I could borrow your wheel wrench for a couple of minutes?" I ask.

"Sure," he says and starts getting out.

"But no sudden moves," I say and let the tip of the gun barrel show above the windowsill.

He doesn't say anything to that one and opens up the

87

hood and pulls out a tool kit and slips out the wheel wrench and closes the hood.

"Just drop it on the ground there," I say.

He does that and climbs back into the Porsche.

"Okay now scram," I say. "I'll leave the thing here for you for when you come back."

He gives me a nice little smile and off they go with a shudder and drive down the road about two hundred yards and then pull over to the side and stop, which sort of pisses me off, some people just don't know when they're not wanted around here.

I slip the gun into my pants pocket and slide out the right door and go around to the trunk where I swing down the continental tire kit which doesn't have a tire in it and unlock the trunk and pull out the spare and jack. I cart all of this around to the front and slip the jack under the front bumper and pump away which is a hell of a lot of work and I swear that one of these days I'm going to get a chauffeur to do this sort of thing. I get the jack up and the tire off and slip on the spare which seems to have enough air in it and tighten everything up and let her down and pile the stuff back into the trunk including the wheel wrench which I decide to keep for all the trouble those jokers are causing me.

Back in the saddle again I feel pretty pooped from all the exercise and think maybe I came close to overdoing it that time, got to watch that. I slip the thing into drive and bounce over a couple of rocks and head back for town. As I round the bend I can see the Porsche making a U-turn and now I wish badly I'd taken a couple of potshots at their tires. It only takes them about a minute to get back on my tail, damn.

About then Chester calls.

"Say boss we've been giving that number—"

"Hang on a minute Chester, I want you to check out the license number of a fairly new Porsche," and I give him the number of my friends behind, "and find out whatever else you can about the car, the bastards are following me."

"Following *you?*"

"That's right Chester."

"Serious. O'Mallollolly's boys?"

"To tell you the truth I'm not sure," I say.

"Okay, just a second boss."

I can hear him relaying the number into another phone.

"Okay boss," he says.

"One other thing before I forget it Chester, and that's O'Mallollolly's limousine which has been towed down to Rex Auto Wrecks where I think Ralph ought to be able to pick it up for a song. All right, what else is new?"

"I'm pretty sure that number you gave me to memorize is a Geneva bank account number."

"Which bank?" I ask.

"Well that's what we don't know. If we can find that out we're all set."

"Go through Roughah's papers with a fine-tooth comb."

"Will do, boss. Now we found out that a guy by the

name of Jonas Smythe has rented a giant tree sloth costume from Mardi Gras Costume Rentals on upper Ninth
Street twice before and has got it rented this very moment. They said he paid thirty-seven dollars to have the
hole in the chest repaired with genuine giant tree sloth
fur flown directly in from New Guinea or somewhere. I've
got Jimmy posted outside to see what he looks like when
he brings it back."

"Good thinking Chester."

"Now I'm beginning to get the impression from Mark
that there's some sort of hitch in the freeway deal."

"What?"

"He's not talking yet, just a hint."

"Mmm," I say.

"You know Mark."

"Yes. Okay now Chester what do you think the chances
are of snatching Roughah's body out of the Police
Morgue?"

"Why boss?"

"O'Mallollolly's going to make the inquest say suicide
no matter what so the only way we can prove he was
murdered is to get the body to the right people."

"Right boss. I think Subcommissioner MacGanymede's
got a foothold in Cold Storage and I'll ask him what can
be done."

"Do that Chester."

I hang up and the Porsche is still on my tail which
really makes me burn, and not just because they follow so
goddamn close. I wonder who the hell they think they

are, tailing me around since it's none of their business
where I go and what I do and I wonder who told them it
was. If O'Mallollolly wants to know where I am, he's got
his ways just like I've got mine and at least when I have
Gifford tail O'Mallollolly he knows how to do it tactfully,
though I am wondering what happened to him. Well, I
think, it must be O'Mallollolly's boys in the Porsche because there isn't anybody else in town who'd do this sort
of thing, and maybe he's doing it for a joke and if so I
decide it's up to me to have the last laugh. I get an idea
and call back Chester.

"Chester I'm switching over to the Kaiser in about ten
minutes. Leave a message for Marge at the Wolverine
Lodge."

"Okay boss."

In a minute I turn left onto the east end of Mirindaranda Road and take my time with no fancy traffic and
signal work so they won't lose me because they've got to
be close if my little plan's going to work. We roll down
Mirindaranda at a fair clip and then I take it real slow on
the right turn onto Songtongob Avenue where I try to
lengthen the gap to about a half block, but not enough to
trap them in the tricky signals. Again I take a slow right
at SWEETE OLDE GRANDMA'S SUGARY PANCAKE HOME-
RESTAURANT onto Kidney Street and go two blocks and
turn left down the alley that runs back of Marge's place
and race up that as fast as I can to the next street, where I
make a quick right turn just as the Porsche enters the
alley.

I whip the Nash around in a U-turn and head back into the alley with my headlights off. I cinch up the safety belt and shove the thing in low and tromp on the accelerator and point the nose on a collision course at the little silver Porsche. Quick, though, the Porsche catches on that I'm running him down and stops and puts it into reverse and starts backing out of the narrow alley. I'm getting close and the Nash is up to thirty and I turn the headlights on high and go *BLAAOUK!* with the air horn which puts the Porsche in such a panic they back into a phone pole and become a sitting duck. *Crash* and that's the end of the Porsche and probably the death blow for my trusty Nash too.

I unfasten the seat belt and spring the door open and from what I can see as I slide out it's going to take my friends a little while to pry themselves out of their tin can in good health or bad. I hotfoot it down the alley to Marge's place and up her back stairs, I hope without being seen or followed, and then unlock her back door with the key she always leaves under a couple of rounds of that artificial plastic dogshit you can buy at your local novelty store.

Inside the kitchen her cat is about to faint or explode so I stop and open a LARGE EXPENSIVE-SIZE CAN of PUSSY-YUM-YUM VITAMINIZED CAT FOOD FOR CAT GOURMETS which stinks to high heaven, but boy does it ever sell. Then I run through the living room and down the stairs and let myself quietly out the front door. The coast is clear, but then it's pretty damn dark out now.

I slip across the lawn to the '55 Kaiser supercharged and am about to climb in when I notice the left front tire is flat as a pancake, which irritates me pretty badly because it happens to be a BIG DADDY LIFETIME EVER-LASTING RETREAD about a month old and they're usually good for at least six months. Today is a bad day for tires I tell myself and get the tire pump out of the trunk. I unscrew the cap and blow that out and screw on the pump nozzle good and tight and start pumping. It's a lot of work and if I had the choice I'd change a tire any day to pumping one up but it so happens the street is really too dark to consider that even though I'm pumping against the theory that the tire's got a slow leak and not that some teen-ager's given it a couple of jabs with his knife.

In spite of not being used to this kind of exercise, I do get the thing pumped up and when I kick it it sounds about like the others, so I figure I'm okay. I stash the pump in the trunk, thoroughly expecting now the five sardines to come around the corner on foot and ask me for a ride, they're that type. No signs, however, and I climb inside the beast which smells like an old couch somebody's turned water on, but then the thing has been shut up and sitting in the sun for weeks now and the fog at night. I fire her up and after one hell of a lot of coughing and missing and smoking out the rear, she finally smooths out and acts like she's ready to be moved, so off we go.

About then I realize the exercise has made me pretty hungry, but not for another Hershey bar, which I don't have anyway. I turn left at the first corner and hit the BEAU CHATEAUX CITY ESTATE HOMES TRACT and take the main street wandering through, lined with trees illuminated by various colors of ground floodlights except green, ending up at the vast sprawl of YOUR LOCALLY OWNED AND RUN BONANZA-BANQUETTE SUPERMARKET. As a matter of fact, it isn't at all locally owned since I don't live around these parts and of course in a neighborhood like B. C. CITY ESTATE HOMES nobody owns anything and nobody knows who owns what they don't which is almost everything.

I steer the Kaiser into the huge floodlighted parking lot which is half the size of the largest runway of the municipal airport and roll along slowly toward the main entrance. There's not one leaf of vegetation on the lot and most people notice that on the long hike from the car to entrance and think what a nice thing it would be to have trees around, and so we very obligingly surround the main entrance with the BONANZA-BANQUETTE GREEN OASIS NURSERY where they can buy a whole forest to take home if they want which some of them need since the B. C. CITY ESTATE HOMES were sold without one leaf of vegetation on them also.

I dock the Kaiser next to the entrance in the G space and step out and walk through the OASIS NURSERY into the main supermarket and around the snack bar that's been put in the way to siphon off the kids, and through the soda fountain with multicolored liquids sloshing around noisily in large conspicuous roundish transparent plastic containers that's supposed to make everybody drool who's been out on that parking lot.

Things are pretty crowded tonight whatever day of the week it is, and I push my way through the shoppers and turnstiles and look for the canned fish section which I can never remember where it is, somewhere over in the corner I think. I grab a shopping cart not because I need one but because I don't want to give people the idea that it's respectable to go through a supermarket without one, and if you've got a cart you've pretty well got to put something in it because you know how much they bounce and rattle when they're empty. Also I want to try out this new kind of cart we've got and so I head for the conspicuous EXPENSIVE FANCY GOURMET FOODS AND DELICACIES DEPARTMENT and trundle along at an average fast shopper's speed. As soon as I hit FANCY FOODS I feel the almost imperceptible drag in the cart wheels which is caused by a magnetic field in the floor actuating tiny magnets which push small abrasive pads against the cart wheels and thus slow the cart and shopper down to a slightly slower than normal browsing rate which is often enough to drag the shopper down to the average buying stance, which is characterized by an instant of total immobility and silence and a reflective look on the face immediately preceding the dancelike gesture which removes the can or whatever from the shelf and drops it into the cart while at the same time already moving on to the next item, or cash register.

I wheel through that and around little traffic jams of shoppers and think the magnets are working well, I was a bit skeptical before. The fish department I find around the corner in the next aisle and spot the little stack of cheapest kippers of some sort and pick up a can and make sure it's got a key on it and then head toward CRACKERS where I pick up a big box of Ritz. That's all I want, so I wheel my way down the aisle and turn left toward the six-items-or-less checkout counter which is a hell of a lot less fancier than the thirty-five checkout counters for more than six items. I roll the cart up and pull out my Ritz crackers and kippers and slide them over to Miss 285 who's clearly the real bitch type we want for six-items-or-less. She claws at the cash register a second and then looks up at me with that special cheap bastard look.

"Anything else, honey?" she asks.

"Nope."

She gives the cash register a last rabbit punch and I slip out a Presidential Voucher pad and write one out for seventy-nine cents and hand it to her. She looks at it and compares the signature with the master form and stamps it and gives me back the carbon and starts reaching for the next six-items-or-less load not even bothering to say thanks, of course she isn't supposed to.

Good girl that one, I think as I hike back to the car, more of her and we'll have six-items-or-less completely stamped out; what doesn't pay ought not to exist, as I always say.

I go out the automatic doors which puts me right by the Kaiser, and there's this checkstand boy sweeping up a bag of rice somebody dropped who watches me go over to the car and step in and as I put the key in the ignition he walks over too.

"Hey," he says, "you'd better get this wreck out of here damn quick, this space is reserved for GASCOYNE."

"It's all right sonnyboy."

"You think? Just get your ass out of here—"

"It's all right I said, I'm GASCOYNE."

He takes a look at the driver's license I shove under his nose but I can tell he's the skeptical kind and I don't have the time to give him the whole proof. I don't get around to these places very often so this sort of thing is common enough. I start up the Kaiser and race the engine to clear it out and shove it in reverse and take my driver's license back. He gives me a mean look for his young age and I pull out of there.

I cruise through the parking lot steering with one hand and ripping the box of Ritz crackers open with the other and then I bounce onto the street and turn left and pull over to the curb to get the can of kippers open which I can't quite manage while driving. I slip the key in and twist the thing open and pick out the little fishes and stoke them in one by one wishing I'd got a box of napkins since I'm out of them. Chewing away I throw a look back at the BONANZA-BANQUETTE which is actually pretty new and think we did a pretty good job on making the thing look three times more expensive than it was to build. We want to make people afraid not to shop there and so we give them the idea that if they don't the thing'll go bankrupt and there'll be an economic depression just around the corner for the whole neighborhood and pretty soon the whole country. Sales went up sharply last week when we spread the rumor the thing wasn't making money, but the truth is the only people not making money are the six neighborhood grocers we put into retirement while getting a fantastic bargain on their unsold goodies.

I finish up the kippers and toss the can out the window and take on some more crackers as I get the Kaiser rolling again, missing a bit more than normal. All of a sudden I wonder where the hell I'm going and feel a little drowsy which is what happens every time I eat dinner though my memory's something that sort of comes and goes. There's this Roughah and O'Mallollolly thing to be cleared up, I know that, but I'm just too tired to think of how far I've got.

Nothing else to do, so I pull back over to the curb and turn off the lights and ignition and push the seat back and hit the hay.

I wake up about ten minutes later and pull the seat forward and turn on the ignition and lights and put the Kaiser into drive. Then I give Chester a ring.

"Hello Chester?"

"No boss, this is Steve."

"Where the hell's Chester?"

"Went out for a late night snack," he says.

"Hell I told him to have his food brought in, what's got into him?"

"Don't ask me, boss."

"Goddamn I'm asking you, pinhead."

"Sorry I don't know, boss. He didn't say anything else."

"That's better. He didn't tell you where Nadine Corell is right now?"

"No boss and I can't make out a word of his shorthand."

"Damn!"

I hang up thinking Chester above all ought to know better than to do something like that but there's not a thing I can do about it at the moment so I decide to run over to the Roughah digs on the chance of finding the Widow Roughah there and seeing if she has anything new to say. I put on the supercharger and whiz up through the VIEWORAMA RIDGE FAMILY HOMES WITH GARDENS TRACT and then down to Mirindaranda Road where I turn right heading straight for the Roughah digs. Traffic's getting lighter every minute and I always look forward to the time when there's nobody else on the street but a few cops and street cleaners and drunks.

Pretty soon I get to the Roughah gate and looking left as far as I can make out the red and white and blue are still in the garage. Lights are on up at Mt. Vernon so somebody must be there. I turn right and leave the Kaiser, which is strangely wheezing, on the street out of sight from the gate or house. I turn off the lights and motor and stash a fistful of crackers into my coat pocket and pop myself out of the car.

Under the cover of darkness I slip through the main gate and turn right and tramp along the big iron fence to the trees and shrubbery which run parallel to the long gravel driveway up to the house. I scramble up through the bushes and it takes me about twenty minutes mainly because some asshole planted a cactus bed which I didn't see until I was in it, causing me to stop ten minutes to pull out the spikes. Finally when I get to the near corner of the house I peek in the windows but there's no sign of life and so I work around the outside and all the rooms on the ground floor are equally empty.

However from somewhere upstairs I hear low-pitched pulsations and I spot the open window that they're coming from on the second floor. I hotfoot it down to the tool shed out back that I've got a key to and unlock it and pull out a tall lightweight aluminium ladder which I tote back and lay against the house below the window. I take off my shoes and cram them into my coat pockets to keep the noise down and then I climb up the ladder to the window and what a sight!

First there's the Widow Roughah stretched out on the bed naked as all hell and second more or less on top of her is the hairy-chested fake giant tree sloth, and I think some people sure like to butter their bread funny. I always thought there was more than meets the eye in that woman and now I know what. But I really feel sorry for the poor bastard inside the sloth suit which must smell like twenty-nine jockstraps in a pressure cooker. But maybe he likes that, you never know.

I watch the show for awhile and the tree sloth keeps wanting to take his claws off and she keeps wanting him to keep them on, but otherwise I don't learn any new tricks from them and get pretty bored and the only thing that keeps me there as long as I stay is that I keep myself busy with a little amateur photography using my Minox.

They finish up and now I figure is the time to go downstairs and make an appearance. I climb down the ladder and carry it back to where it belongs and go to the front door and pound on it and ring the doorbell at the same time. After about ten minutes the Widow Roughah opens the door in that slinky black gown of hers.

"What do you want GASCOYNE?" she asks with not very much interest evident.

"Are you alone?" I ask and nudge the door open wider and squeeze through.

"Yes."

"You're lying again Nadine."

We walk into the living room which is the scene of the crime.

"Yes," she says thoughtfully, "I am."

"Well?"

"I have my reasons," she says.

"Name one."

"Sometimes I just like to lie, that's all."

"All right. Let's get down to brass tacks. Do you know anything about a number with eight digits in it?" I ask, fingering the little gold coin in my pants pocket.

She counts on her fingers up to eight. "No, do you?"

"It doesn't ring a bell or anything like that?" I ask.

"What's the number?"

"Well," I say, "it really doesn't matter what the number is if it doesn't mean anything."

"Give me the number," she says, "and I'll see if it rings a bell."

"No I can't do that Nadine."

"Well give me part of it then."

"What for?" I ask.

"Curiosity."

"All right, one of the digits is nine."

"*Nine?*"

"Yes, nine."

"*Nine. Which* digit?" she asks.

"Well I just agreed to give a digit but I didn't agree to tell you which digit."

"Oh don't be silly GASCOYNE. If I had all the numbers except one digit I wouldn't need to know where it went, would I?"

"Somebody might have given you the digits in the wrong order," I say.

"Still, knowing where the nine goes wouldn't help all that much."

"It might," I say. "Supposing someone gave you the eight digits in the proper sequence but without telling you which digit began the number. Thus if I told you that nine was the third digit then all you would have to do to restore the proper number would be to count three to the left."

"Is nine the third digit?" she asks.

"No."

"Please GASCOYNE."

"No."

"Now look here," she says, "I'm paying you to find out little bits of information like this."

"But I am the judge of which information is relevant to the case, Miss Corell, and don't you ever forget that."

She glares at me.

"Then," I go on, "an eight-digit number with nine as one or more of the digits *does* ring a bell."

"No," she says, "it doesn't ring a goddamn thing."

"Pshaw," I say.

She goes and flings herself stomach down on a sofa not far from the bat-winged bloodstain.

"Now Miss Corell it has come to my attention that there is probably in existence a life insurance policy purchased by your late husband which is estimated at about a million bucks with you presumably as the beneficiary," I say as if I know it to be dead certain. "Is that right?"

"Close enough."

"And who has a copy of the policy at the moment?"

"Only I," she says.

"Might I be able to examine it someday?" I ask.

"Not on your life."

"Very well. If that's the way you feel."

"It is," she says.

"Now then. Is my assumption correct that you have

hired me Miss Corell only in order to have the hypothesis of suicide put in serious doubt, if not disproven entirely, so as to permit you to benefit from the insurance benefits?"

"That's correct."

"Then you don't really give a damn about the character or exact identity of the murderer or hypothetical murderer."

"Murderer," she corrects. "No, I don't."

"Thus you would have no objections to a frame-up."

"None whatever."

"Is there anyone in particular you would like to see framed up?" I ask.

"I can't think of anyone at the moment but I'll think about it and let you know."

"I'd sure appreciate that Miss Corell. Now the next thing—"

Just then the doorbell rings loudly and there's pounding on the door. Nadine though keeps laying there tummy down on the sofa looking wistfully at the bat-shaped bloodstain.

"Well," I say, "aren't you going to answer it?"

Finally she gets up and brushes back her long black hair and goes down the hall to answer the door and comes back chatting with a young fellow about twenty-five dressed in a dark suit, and he'd be one of those clean-cut guys except the trouble is he's got what looks to me exactly like an octopus tentacle hanging out his left ear, about nine inches long I'd say and sort of waving around aimlessly. About then I think this Widow Roughah sure runs around with the funniest people I've ever seen and maybe old Rufus did pull the trigger after all, I don't blame him one bit.

"GASCOYNE I'd like you to meet Jeremy Armstrong, an old friend of mine," says Nadine in a hostesslike way that reminds me of the good old days.

Then as she's showing us where to sit down she manages to get between us and looks at me and mouths in a whisper, "Just pretend like everything's all right!"

"Well Mr. Armstrong what do you do for a living?" I ask as we all sit down.

"At the moment nothing. I've just come back from the wars. . . ."

"What wars?"

"Well I'm sorry I can't say sir," he says.

"Oh *those* wars. I understand."

"Cigarette?"

"No," I say, "I don't smoke. I don't drink either."

Though right now I sure could use something because that octopus tentacle waving around is a little more than I can take. But he doesn't seem to mind it at all. Funny what you can get used to. Of course what I want to know is where the other seven tentacles are and what they're doing.

"Well Mr. Armstrong," I ask just as soon as I can think up a question, "how do you intend to make your living now that you're back from the wars?"

"I hope sir to find a position."

The old tentacle is flying around so much now it's making his head jerk back and forth.

"What sort?" I ask.

"An office position sir."

He looks at me strangely and then stiffens up and his eyes jerk to a straight ahead position.

"Give it a peanut," he says hoarsely and adding, "please."

The end of the tentacle is now curled around like an elephant's trunk which must be its feeding position.

"Give it a peanut!" Nadine whispers at me urgently.

I rummage through my pockets.

"I don't have any peanuts. All I've got are Ritz crackers."

"Give it a peanut," croaks Jeremy Armstrong.

"We've got to give it a peanut!" says Nadine.

"What'll happen if we don't?"

"I don't know but it's pretty awful."

I begin to get the picture. Armstrong's still stuck in his trancelike state but the octopus arm is getting a little impatient and waving around with a hell of a lot of gusto.

"Get the butler," I whisper to Nadine.

She reaches over the sofa and pulls the bell cord. About then Armstrong falls off his chair and doubles up on the rug with the tentacle making like it's smoothing his hair.

"Damn!" says Nadine.

"What?"

"I forgot. The butler's dead."

"There must be other servants," I say.

"Yes!"

She pushed a little button at the base of a table lamp, revealing a round illuminated dial reading from left to right *Butler, Upstairs Maid, Downstairs Maid, Chauffeur, Gardener, Gamekeeper, Chef, Lawyer.*

"Who would have peanuts?" she asks.

"Give it a peanut," Armstrong moans.

"Try the chef," I say.

She turns the gadget to *Chef* and pushes a button.

Now the tentacle starts taking nasty jerks at Armstrong's hair which makes him shudder.

The chef walks in the door sleepy-eyed and holding up his pajama bottoms with one hand.

"Man, get me a bag of salted peanuts this very instant!" Nadine shrieks in a state of near collapse.

The chef runs out the door and I get up to make sure he does in fact go after the peanuts but in a second he comes back in and I grab the box of peanuts away from him and Nadine snatches it from me. About this point the octopus tentacle starts picking Armstrong's nose which is pretty disgusting. Nadine rips off the cellophane and the box top and pulls out a peanut and smashes the shell and picks out a solitary nut which she splits in half and offers to the tentacle. The tentacle sniffs at it a moment and then gingerly takes it and thrusts it into Armstrong's ear-hole. Finally the tentacle curls up in Armstrong's ear as best the space allows anyway and appears to go to sleep, which is what the rest of Armstrong is now doing with very loud snores.

Gascoyne

"Well what do you know about that?" I say.

"GASCOYNE you've got to do something to help the poor boy."

"Who is he?"

"We were lovers before I married Roughah for his money. I haven't seen Jeremy since the day of my marriage, I mean he came to see me as soon as he heard of Roughah's death. He was here this afternoon, again with that horrible thing sticking out of his ear."

"Where did he ever pick it up?" I ask.

"I don't know. He obviously got it during the wars but of course he can't say anything about the wars, you know how they are. But there's something very strange back of all this GASCOYNE."

"I'll say. Uncanny. Weird. Unearthly."

"Awful. Can you do something GASCOYNE? I mean the poor boy can't go on like this. And what if it spreads?"

"Grows larger you mean?"

"No. What if it's contagious?"

"Mmm. That would be serious," I say.

"For my sake GASCOYNE do something."

"Love him do you?"

"Yes," she says.

"I'll see what I can do. It'll cost you a little extra you know."

"I'll pay anything GASCOYNE to have him freed from that thing."

"You know we could just cut it off," I suggest.

She shudders. "I couldn't think of it."

"Look. I'll take care of your boyfriend here and get the insurance money all for the bargain price of a hundred and twenty-five thou."

"Anything GASCOYNE anything!"

"All right. Now I've got an in with a man who knows about these things and it'll take me a couple of hours to get out and back to see him. In the meantime I want you to put Jeremy here in a well-heated room with lots of salted peanuts. And don't let anybody in or out of that room, understand?"

"Yes GASCOYNE. And thanks."

"Don't mention it."

I slip out the front door and hike down the gravel driveway and get about halfway down when I remember I forgot to give her the third degree on the sloth suit upstairs, I'm getting absentminded in my old age but then I can't say that things going on at the moment are exactly simple and easy to keep track of, lucky I've got what memory I've got.

I get back to the Kaiser and climb in and get her rolling though she doesn't want to much and then give Chester a ring.

"Chester what the hell do you think you're trying to do by running out of the office at a time like this to *eat?*"

"It wasn't only that boss, I had to get some pills."

"Pills?"

"Yeah, I got some shooting pains in my chest."

"Hell I told you you shouldn't smoke."

"It isn't that part of my chest."

"Well all right all I want you to do next time you want
to go out is just let me know, even if it's just to go piss in
the toilet next door. I don't mind shooting pains Chester
but a job's a job."

"Sure boss," he says.

"All right what's the latest dope?"

"First the Porsche you asked about was sold out-of-state
and licensed here only this month under the name of Fritz
Schmidt, whose address turns out to be a vacant lot."

"Strange," I say.

"That's all we know. Now we still haven't found out
what happened to Gifford who was trailing O'Mallollolly
but what's-his-name trailing Dmitri saw O'Mallollolly go
into Dmitri's place with Nancy and Nadine Roughah earlier this evening."

"That must have been about the time I was busy with
the Porsche crowd. Well Chester get Willy or somebody
back on O'Mallollolly's tail. At this hour he's either at Police Tower or home, and I want reports every half hour if
possible, got it? The sooner I know what he's up to the
happier I'll be."

"Right boss."

"What else is there?"

"Not much good," he says. "No word on the jeeps yet.
And we're still waiting to hear from Mark. Something's
bad in the wind on the housing-tract–freeway deal but
what it is he's not giving yet."

"Hell, Mark ought to know better than to try to hold out on me, what's got into him?"

"Don't know boss. Louis is now overdue on the TJ package."

"What's it worth?" I ask.

"About two and a half million."

"Hmm," I say.

"Yeah it'll be pretty hot if he gets nabbed."

"I'll say. Well what's the latest on Roughah's body?"

"Afraid we've been anticipated there boss. O'Mallollolly's got it set up that nobody can touch it with a ten-foot pole and MacGanymede's pretty glum about switching bodies."

"See what you can do Chester."

"Sure boss," he says with a voice that sounds a little funny.

"You all right?"

"Just a little tired boss, like I said."

"A cup of fresh coffee can do wonders Chester."

"I'll try it boss."

I hang up about the time Mangoldia Avenue runs into the Quadrastate High Rise Skyway on-ramp. I turn left with the green arrow and snap on the supercharger going up the ramp and get her up to seventy as I merge into the Skyway and then whip over to the fast lane and shoot her up to eighty, but I can't stay there because the front wheel begins shimmying like death so I push her up to eighty-five which is a big improvement though probably not too good for the hamster mill up front. So with a little peace and quiet at last I decide it's time for some thinking. There's one thing I really want to know and that's why O'Mallollolly's trying to cover up the murder and why he's doing it so energetically instead of just sitting on the body back in Police Tower. He might well be having trouble buying the Widow Roughah off because he's got to top the insurance thing, a cool million. Well, one idea comes up in my mind and makes a little sense but not much, and that's that O'Mallollolly bumped Roughah off for one of twenty reasons and is now covering it up because he wants to win the next election in a couple of months all by himself and without any help. But he ought to know that not even George Washington himself can get himself elected to a public office in this town unless he's got the right man behind him, and if he doesn't know that now he's going to have to learn it the hard way sooner than he thinks, starting any day of the week from now on. But I just don't think O'Mallollolly could be quite that dumb. He got elected himself back in '59 because poor old MacWigo tried to go it alone, it can't be done.

But at least the Widow Roughah is beginning to see the value of telling the truth now and then and there's reason to suppose this might become a habit. What I really want to see is that insurance policy to make sure she's on the level about that and because somewhere in the back of my mind Roughah and insurance policy are rubbing together in an unusual way and I want to know why.

Now the little gold disk with the eight-digit number on it is still a mystery and judging from what has happened so far it's the key to a hell of a lot more than meets the eye at first glance. The number's trying to say something but it's just not coming through very clear. I take the little coinlike thing out of my pocket and hold it up in the skyway glare so as to be able to read the number: 95400329. I notice an odd symmetry in it as it begins with a nine and ends with a nine and has two zeros smack in the middle with the remaining four numbers being two pairs of neighboring numbers, five-four and three-two. What's it trying to say? Whatever it is must be pretty damn significant.

About then some idiot coming the opposite direction on the Skyway jumps the center strip and goes end over end clear across into our slow lane and piles into a moving van and the whole shooting match plows through the side railing and sails off the Skyway into the Skyway View Homes for Fast-Living Families Tract and the last I see of them is an orange glow down below out the rear-view. Somebody down there's going to have something to talk about over breakfast. That's about the fanciest one I've seen in a long time and I get to see quite a few because one of the advantages of being on the road all the time is you pretty often find yourself in a front-row seat for freeway spectaculars.

Suddenly out of the blue a couple of pieces slam together like they always belonged that way. *The butler did it*, as O'Mallollolly said, and why not? Grant, the old fool, is dead and of course he couldn't have done it but he's in no position to argue and now all I have to do is get Grants' body and make up fingerprints and a little evidence here and there and the Widow Roughah gets her insurance money and me my cut, like shooting ducks in a barrel. That's a solution to make everybody happy and it tidies up one end of the Roughah business real nice. Of course I'm still wanting to know who really did it but that's something there's no real rush about. Just then the phone rings. It's Marge.

"Hi Marge, where are you calling from?"

"The Wolverine Lodge dear, and I've got a beautiful room. View of the pine trees, the lake, Mount Pastiche with the sun coming up all over it, everything."

"For how much?"

"Twenty-five dear, very cheap."

"Well I don't know about that. That sounds pretty expensive to me Marge. Didn't they have any cheaper rooms?"

"Oh just one for fifteen practically in the basement," she says.

"Did you look at it?"

"Of course not dear. The nice man at the desk told me frankly it just wasn't suitable. Right above the boiler room and just under the kitchen," she says.

"Just the same you shouldn't take other people's word about these things Marge, it may have been a perfectly nice cosy little room and all you really needed was a bed for the night. They just wanted you to use one of their expensive rooms. Is that twenty-five dollars for a single?"

"Oh no dear, it's a double."

"A double? What did you want a double for?"

"They didn't have any singles left," she says.

"Oh. How was your trip up?"

"Oh just marvelous."

"No more car trouble?" I ask.

"Not a bit. And it wouldn't have mattered anyway."

"Oh?"

"Well dear I was very lucky. It seems that the nice boy who keeps the bar at Crankcase Grade Summit had to come up to Wolverine Camptown to pick up his car which broke down there."

"Yes?"

"Well so I offered him a ride, and in fact I was so tired yesterday afternoon and really rather smashed that I just let him do the driving and I sat back and relaxed and enjoyed the scenery."

"Well now Marge really I don't think you should carry around strange men. After all that car is worth almost six thousand dollars and we can't have it insured for everybody's uncle to drive, and you know how these teen-agers are."

"He's not a teen-ager dear," she says. "He's twenty-three and quite grown up."

"Did he drive safely?"

"Oh yes."

"How long did it take you from the summit to the lodge?"

"Oh let me see now. About three hours," she says.

"Three hours? He must have driven very slowly."

"Oh no dear, we stopped for a little picnic for a couple of hours, the weather was so nice at the other side of the pass."

"Umm. What are you doing now Marge?"

"Just lying in bed watching the sun come up, you know, and digesting my breakfast. The air is so good up here that all you want to do is lie around and breathe. Exhilarating!"

"Well now Marge don't forget what I sent you up there for in the first place."

"Yes, I'll get up to Condor's Crag late this afternoon I expect. At the moment I'm just too exhausted. My whole body just sort of aches all over, very pleasant—"

"Whatever from Marge?"

"The altitude dear. Its effects are quite penetrating."

"Funny I've never felt that before."

"Well that's just the way you are," she says.

"Okay Marge I've got to go."

I hang up pretty peeved at her for throwing my money around like that and also acting as if she's on vacation and not on an errand. Time and money don't grow on trees and that's one thing she ought to know by now, and of course it's very illuminating about her the way she starts slowing down and spending money as soon as she's out of sight. Well she'll get hell when she gets back as if she didn't know it.

Pretty soon I reach the place where the Skyway comes back down to the ground on the edge of the wheatlands and where you can first see the towers of Fort Frigge Army Base which everybody in town thinks is a big storage dump for things they're going to use in the next war but the place is really a cover for NON-PROFIT DEFENSIVE ZOOLOGICAL WARFARE SYSTEMS INCORPORATED which is one of these government contractors with special milking privileges because we were able to talk the government into believing there was nobody else around with enough brains to do the job, no little trick that one was. Most of the joint is stuck under the ground or in places that look like warehouses and we've got about five thousand people working there secretly, but so that nobody gets suspicious and wondering why so many Ph.Ds in defensive zoological warfare are in the area they've put up a big fancy Agriculture Department Testing Station just down the road and they let it out that since there's nothing these days for the zoological warfare people to do they give them work on peaceful plants and animals.

The Fort Frigge off-ramp sign pops up and I pump the brakes and slip over into the slow lane and shoot down the ramp and turn left at the bottom and roll through the underpass and wind up at the gendarme's office at the Fort Frigge Main Gate. A corporal takes down my license number and takes a gander at my driver's license and gives me a visitor's pass and waves me through. They're pretty casual about letting you in so they won't attract too much attention but they're damn careful about letting you out if they let you out at all, and they always pretend they don't know you.

I slip the Kaiser into the G slot beside a huge building that's supposed to have nothing in it but mothballed jeep pistons but the place really sits on top of the whole NON-PROFIT DEFENSIVE ZOOLOGICAL WARFARE SYSTEMS ADMINISTRATION AND LABORATORIES which go straight down into the ground for a hell of a long ways.

I climb out of the car and hoof it over to the main entrance of the building and give my visitor's pass to an army security Pfc who gives me a little form to fill out. I tell him I haven't got my glasses with me so he fills it out for me and pushes a button and opens a wooden hatch in the floor behind his desk and helps me into the hole which is almost too small for me. I get my feet planted firmly on the wooden rungs of the ladder, and since I've been through this about ten times before I don't really mind that he's picked my pockets, they give it all back to you when you leave.

I start climbing down the wooden ladder and he closes the hatch over my head. I've got about fifty feet down below which is enough space and time for them to take pictures and weigh me and measure me and take X-rays and fingerprints without me supposed to notice anything unusual and in fact I wouldn't even know what they're doing if a friend inside hadn't told me all about it. And of course the rungs are unevenly spaced so you've got to keep your mind on what you're doing if you don't want to break your neck.

I reach the bottom of the ladder with a lot of splinters in my hands and kick myself for forgetting the gloves I always mean to bring. The ladder ends in a small flood-lighted room which is where army security leaves off and NONPROFIT DEFENSIVE ZOOLOGICAL takes over. One wall of the thing which is about ten by twenty-five feet is completely covered with a security poster with letters in white against black seven feet tall reading "SHHHHH!" and underneath in very small white letters SECURITY IS YOUR BUSINESS. ALSO YOUR JOB. . . . Why they put it here I don't know since the regular employees come in an easier way but maybe they couldn't find anybody who'd have the thing in his office, pretty clear why.

I go through a small door left into the reception office and a girl behind a typewriter is already looking over the stuff the Pfc sent down and the photographs and X-rays and things taken on the way down the hole.

"Mr. GASCOYNE," she says in that snotty voice these typing chicks sometimes get, "I see you've gained two pounds since you were last here."

"That's right."

"Why?" she asks looking at me through thick glasses and with poisonous bright lipstick and a golden ball-point pen held up in the air at an angle like she doesn't give a living fart whether the X goes in the Yes box or the No box, I hate the type and she ought to know better than to ask me personal questions. I'll have to fire this number.

"Constipation," I say.

Her glassy wet eyes twitch an upper lid or two and her pen descends to the paper like a pin into a voodoo doll.

"We must be very careful you know Mr. GASCOYNE. Very careful indeed."

Moments like this I pride myself on saying nothing at all. She goes and stamps a pass form and lovingly crunches a number slip onto it with a stapler that she bangs like she was delivering a fatal judo punch and then she grinds a finger into a button like she's hoping somehow it'll make a bomb go off somewhere.

After a second the secretary of Dr. Phialson, the man I want to see, clanks in and clips a little red SHHH! badge to my lapel which is to remind people I don't have a security clearance, not that I need one, and it even glows in the dark in case they have a power failure down here. Then she puts the loop end of a long chain around my neck and puts the other end around hers which is to make sure that an uncleared person such as I am or any other visitor is always with his escort. All the chains themselves have a special security classification and must be kept in safes when not in use which enables the number of visitors in the place at one time to be monitor-confirmed and also if somebody finds a chain laying around it's pretty damn clear something fishy's going on somewhere.

When we get all harnessed up we start to pull out of

the reception office and I turn around to give Miss Poison a last nasty look and she looks up and makes a grimace and sticks out her tongue and goes *"Phffsst!"*

"Grrfgh!" I reply with an appropriate gesture and march out.

We enter a hallway about twenty feet wide and a half-mile long and walk down it a ways and go past another security poster which shows in bright blue the mouth of a man sneezing with germ droplets flying everywhere with the caption *"Keep Your Mouth Shut"* with the usual pitch about security underneath.

"Turn left here," says Miss Chain.

"Thanks for warning me."

We clank around a corner and go down a narrow corridor a ways until we get to another big hallway and turn right and run smack into what looks like all hell breaking loose and about to mow us down at the same time. Miss Chain yanks the chain and we whip back around the corner for protection but I peek over her head and look at what's coming. The first thing that runs by looks like a cross between a large crocodile and a boa constrictor on eight legs with TOP SECRET stenciled on its side screaming its head off and probably moving at about 20 mph. Then right on its tail comes a small flock of jabbering white doves that keep crashing into the walls and lights but still moving down the hall pretty damn fast. Suddenly one of them shrieks especially loud and they all start crapping all over the place but the funny thing is when the turds hit

121

the floor or anything solid they explode in a bright red flame burning very large holes in the walls and floors, I wonder what they've been fed.

A black cloud of some little insect whizzes by next leaving behind a bad smell that makes my eyes water and makes me think I'm going to lose my last night's sardine dinner but the smell goes away pretty fast. Then right off, this huge white fluffy round thing about seven feet in diameter comes staggering down the hallway on four tiny little feet underneath and then I see its little bitty face right square in the middle of this round ball and I realize the damn thing's a white rabbit with a weight problem. It sort of bounces from one side of the hall to the other making the walls shake and then this secretary steps out across the hall to see what all the commotion is about and the large round white rabbit trips and knocks her down and rolls right over her and keeps on rolling down the hall out of sight while the secretary crawls back into her door.

Just a second later four guys in white coats and gloves and masks rush by like bats out of hell followed by a gun bearer, and a character with a foam fire extinguisher putting out the little fires. Next comes a little man dressed in black, nosing around everywhere and then he sees me and my Sннн!! badge and comes over and says without even introducing himself or trying to find out who I am, "You have just committed a serious security violation by watching what passed pass."

So then I remember he's the security officer.

"Now I want you to relax," he says looking me in the

eye, "just relax and look me in the eyes. That's it. Now we all have bad dreams now and then and that's just what you've had."

"Sure," I say just to make the guy feel better, though he ought to know who I am and that I'm a busy man and don't have time for dreams of any kind. He babbles on like that for a few minutes while Miss Chain caresses the back of my neck until I agree in a counterfeit sleepy tone that I haven't seen a damn thing. He shakes my hand and runs off and Miss Chain and I go on our way. All I can think is that if I were a taxpayer I'd sure be pissed off at the poor state of organization in this joint, but of course the secret of getting profits out of these nonprofit things is to get the government so confused they don't know where the money goes and pretty soon they don't care either.

We turn a couple of corners and run past a guy killing flies with a bugbomb and then step into an office and old Miss Chain picks up a little wooden knocker and gives a big brass gong a whack. There are about ten girls typing and when they hear the noise they all look up from their typewriters and start pulling big *SHHH!* hoods, which are white with red lettering and tiny air holes, over their desks and bodies and heads and zip themselves up inside and that way conceal all the classified material laying around. We cross through them and go into the private office of Doc Phialson who's in charge of the whole shooting match and he's at his desk asleep over the comics section of the morning *Times*.

"Dr. Phialson?" says Miss Chain. "Oh Doctor?"

He's clearly a deep sleeper and so she gives the desk a little push and he opens his eyes and raises his head and mumbles, "Quitting time is it already?" Then he sees me and says, "GASCOYNE!"

I almost forget that it's a security violation for two people of different security classifications to shake hands and so does he but we stop in time.

"GASCOYNE! Sit down!"

Well I go and sit right down in the chair beside me forgetting completely about Miss Chain and so I give her a nasty jerk on the neck which throws her against the wall with a crash that really rattles her marbles and I stand up to help her but damn if she doesn't fall to the floor which pulls me off my feet and I end up on the floor too under the chair I was sitting on two seconds before and bruised all over the place.

"Sorry," I say.

"That's all right," she says, "it happens all the time."

We make it back on our feet and Miss Chain passes her end of the chain to Doc who loops the end over his neck and then disconnects the thing in the middle and plugs my end into a special socket on his desk in front of me. Miss Chain staggers out of the room, what a nasty job she's got, must be a tough bitch all right.

"Well GASCOYNE what the hell are you doing down here?"

"Well I'll tell you."

So I tell him about Nadine's boyfriend with the ear trouble.

"That's a new one," he says, " a one-legged octopus."

"Says he picked it up in the wars."

"Did he now? Well he's lucky to get back from the wars at all. Not many come back, you know. They like to use them up. Saves money and time and they learn a lot in the field. Can't have a lot of boys coming back who haven't had the full treatment, and that doesn't leave much choice."

"Can this thing be cured?" I ask.

"Presumably not. Otherwise they wouldn't have sent him back." He picks up a fine wire-mesh cage with a spider in it and tosses it from hand to hand. "However it would be worth trying a three-time daily rinse with a very strong solution of Tide detergent, the washday miracle. Also I should recommend mashing up a half peanut and adding to it a small quantity of aspirin or Miltown, but most of all I'd have the boy run out and buy himself a very large hat."

"You think it's that way?"

"Indeed I do GASCOYNE. These wars are frightful things." He keeps tossing the cage back and forth and then stops. "You see here one of our most recent failures."

"Oh?"

"You see here inside a female *Latrodectus mactans,* commonly known as the black widow spider, which of course we have succeeded in making far more deadly than dear old Ma Nature ever was able to, bless her heart. But now we are stumped by a pedagogical problem which is how to make it attack people and how to find people who don't mind this sort of thing or who don't matter. Just can't swing this on our eight-figure budget. This little mother has already cost us over four hundred thousand. I'm now heading an interdepartmental department which starts with earthworms."

"Earthworms?" I ask.

"Well actually the group includes earthworms, snails, slugs and other low-lying sticky fauna. One would never suspect that the lowly earthworm could be used as an instrument of war and holocaust, would one?"

"Never."

"Well that's what we felt until a little while ago. Then we developed this strain of extremely virile and prolific earthworms, three times fatter and twice as long as the regular size, and with a reproductive cycle not only three times shorter but also producing three times the offspring. Now supposing we were to seed the enemy farmlands with these extra-large worms which because they live underground are protected from insecticides, et cetera, except those that also kill crops. Now because of the excessive number of these beasts which would soon be produced, the enemy would first find his farmlands prospering extraordinarily because of the manner in which earthworms enrich the earth. The later effects however are most interesting. You have undoubtedly heard of *Merula migratoria*."

"No," I say.

He leans back and takes a piece of chalk and draws a picture of a bird on the blackboard.

"On this continent it is more usually called the robin redbreast, which is a slightly different bird in Europe. However as you know the enemy has adopted the robin as its national bird because of its red front and the five-and ten-year plans now stress the importance of increasing robin production to catch up with whoever happens to be ahead at the moment.

"Well now to continue. As you know robins like earthworms. The bigger the better. In fact we are presently developing a very prolific strain of robin, three times larger than any robin now known to exist. Well now in the first year of Operation Earthworm, earthworm production under enemy territory will jump ahead by leaps and bounds, bringing on a bumper robin crop the next year, robins which of course will be of this new variety. Now, you have undoubtedly heard of *Felis domestica* or *Felis catus.*"

"No," I say.

He draws what looks to me like a cat on the blackboard.

"More commonly known as the domesticated carnivore which we call the house cat, the common house cat. Now it is a well-known fact that cats like to catch robins and this situation is aided by the fact that robins must be on the ground in order to catch earthworms, though confidentially our department is working on a flying earthworm."

"What for?"

"Strictly a terror weapon. Now of course we will have

to develop a larger strain of house cats to catch the large robins. With this comes the twist of sheer genius. The CIA has found out that there are thirty-eight million house cats on enemy territory with a net increase of seventeen percent a year. Now we project a larger strain of house cat which like the earthworms and robins will be three times larger than the old model and so forth. CIA Market Research has indicated that the three-times-larger house cat is precisely what the average enemy housewife wants this very moment. That is, by the subtle, covert and clandestine introduction of these new cats so as to give the enemy the impression that they are a spontaneous generation of their ideology, very shortly they will become all the rage and very quickly the thirty-eight-million-plus old smaller house cats will be superannuated, purged and liquidated. Now with the large new house cat in circulation, what is going to happen?"

"Beats me."

"Very simple. Because these new cats are larger, more powerful and faster, they will quickly decimate the rat and mice populations, giving the grain crop a boost it has never had before. All right, at this stage the situation is this: fat earthworms, fat robins, fat cats, bumper grain crop. Now just imagine what will happen when we introduce our Micro-Mouse."

"What's that?"

"A mouse three times smaller but three times more prolific than the ordinary house mouse." He draws a very small mouse on the blackboard. "Now this mouse is so small that the very large house cats will hardly be able to see it let alone catch it with their very large claws. And the Micro-Mouse because of its very light weight and relatively heavy fur can be dropped from an altitude of almost a hundred miles, almost literally rained down. You see the point."

"Well no not exactly."

"Well the Air Force is developing a special twenty-ton Pregnant Micro-Mouse Non-Recoverable Transport and Distribution Satellite, the PMMNRTDS for short, that will carry over seven million Micro-Mice, slightly over six million of which will land safely in enemy territory. Well now the complete reproductive cycle of these Micro-Mice is a classified secret of a classification which in itself is Cosmic Top Secret, and only two men in this world know the length of the Micro-Mouse Reproductive Cycle, the MMRC for short."

"Who?"

"The mouse expert who invented the Micro-Mouse— and the President."

"You don't say."

"But it's pretty common knowledge that the MMRC takes about a day, conception to birth."

"Good God!"

"Astounding, isn't it? Now all seven million of these Micro-Mice will be of necessity pregnant females, timed to deliver their young upon touching down in enemy farmlands. Six million, that is those who survive the excursion, six million times twenty offspring makes an almost instantaneous total of one hundred and twenty-six million Micro-Mice, and put them in the Ukrainian Breadbasket and what do you get?"

"Well . . ."

"No grain. No bread. No corn. Nothing. Just eating Micro-Mice and frustrated extra-large cats." Doc pulls out a Camel and lights it nervously. "Of course, there's a rub."

"What's that?"

"Once even one pregnant Micro-Mouse is out, there's nothing anybody can do to stop it."

"What about regular old-fashioned house cats?" I ask.

"They can delay the explosion for perhaps a year, perhaps much less."

"So . . ."

"Yes you see. If just one pregnant Micro-Mouse were to get out of Fort Frigge we would of necessity have to turn into a nation of mouse hunters devoting our complete gross national product of five hundred billion dollars to stamping out the little bastards. Much more dangerous than H-bombs."

"How many are here?"

"With constant liquidation we keep the population down to a million. That sounds high but it isn't—we have to control and perfect the strain and at the moment we're trying to find that magic ingredient that will make them so distasteful to even ordinary house cats they won't even bother to look at them. But every now and then I get the feeling that one of them is going to escape and then the mouse will be out of the bag, so to speak."

"I suppose that's true."

"Statistically inevitable."

"I imagine the enemy would pay quite a pile for a pregnant Micro-Mouse."

"Quite," says Doc. Then he whispers, "The highest offer so far is nine hundred grand."

"Not bad."

Doc leans over the desk a little closer.

"Well as I see it," he says, "one of these days a Micro-Mouse is going to make a break and of course its descendants will be running around the enemy embassy before you can yell mouse, so why not do what's going to happen in the first place and make a little profit on it?"

"Nothing wrong with that."

"Okay GASCOYNE if you can get me one-point-five million for them I'll give you forty percent."

"Fifty on this one," I say, "after all you get sixty percent of the regular NON-PROFIT ZOOLOGICAL SYSTEMS profits."

"Forty," he insists.

"Fifty."

"All right, fifty," he says.

Doc opens his desk drawer and pulls out a glass jar like the kind they put mayonnaise in, with a red screw-top with holes punched in it, and inside I can make out a couple of very tiny gray mice running around the leaves and straw and cotton. He wraps the jar up in the comics section of the *Times* and drops it in his briefcase and then he pulls a little paper bag from his desk and opens it up and shoves it in my face, it's filled with wheat.

"You are to insert the grains into the largest hole one by one. Under no circumstances are you to unscrew the top."

Then he pulls out two old perfume atomizers, one of them filled with a pink liquid, the other with a green.

"This pinkish one contains a liquefied cyanide compound which you are to spray into the jar if things get out of hand or if there's an emergency, and the other contains a virus to which the two pair of Micro-Mice in the jar are immune but not their offspring. This will enable you to keep the population down. Any questions?"

"No Doc."

He puts all the junk in his briefcase and hooks up the chain between us again and we head out the office around a corner to employees' reception where we have to wait a couple of minutes until my personal effects and valuables arrive and when they do I'm happy to find the little gold coin among them though some underpaid government employee lifted a grand of the three grand the Widow Roughah gave me and I'm a little pissed off about that.

Doc and me shoot up to ground level in the elevator and they let us out of the building without even looking in Doc's briefcase and also out of the base. I drive Doc through the underpass to the FORT FRIGGE BIG DADDY SERV-UR-SELPH STATION across the freeway where he's getting his car greased. I stash the Micro-Mice in the glove compartment and drop him off.

"For God's sake be careful GASCOYNE," he says. "One false step and we're all finished, us human beings!"

"I get it."

After I dump Doc I zoom back under the underpass and pull over to the curb in front of one of those old-fashioned grimy little grocery stores and leave the motor running in the Kaiser while I hop out and duck in for a couple of pounds of bananas for breakfast because I'm getting damn hungry all of a sudden. The old lady inside overcharges for the things in the first place and then to make matters really bad goes and weighs part of her left boob with them which makes me so burning mad I lift a pack of Wrigley's from the counter while she dumps the bananas into a sack, though I still think she comes out about three cents ahead on the deal and I make a mental note to look into plopping a BONANZA-BANQUETTE SUPER-MARKET down across the street, that'll teach her.

I climb back into the Kaiser and throw it in drive and turn left up the Skyway on-ramp and floor it with the supercharger on. I hit the slow lane about sixty and merge in just in front of a gas truck and dodge over to the fast lane and wind her up to eighty-five and start unpeeling the bananas. There's something about munching bananas helps my thinking machinery and then too there's nothing quite like dangling banana peels out the window and having them whipped from your fingers by the wind. I let one go and give Chester a ring.

133

"Chester what's up?"

"First, Flash Fingers did a great job with the WESTBINDER BRANCH BANK. The whole place burned up and there isn't a scrap of paper left there."

"Good. Anybody hear what the tax man had to say?"

"Yeah," he says, "he said it was a put-up job."

"Sure everybody knows that but can he prove it?"

"He'd be a genius if he could."

"Right. What else?" I ask.

"Let's see . . ."

There's a hell of a long pause so I say, "You there Chester?"

"Sure boss, just a little drowsy, sorry."

"All right. Well anyway what else is new?"

"Oh. Those guys in the Porsche don't work for O'Mallollolly and don't seem to even live in the state."

"Hmm. You *sure* they're not under O'Mallollolly?"

"Not according to Al in Personnel."

"Can you trust him?" I ask.

"Always have boss."

"All right, keep looking. What else is there?" I ask. Old Chester sounds pretty sluggish this morning.

"What's-his-name's back in town, Fernando."

"Well, well."

"Yeah boss. He wants to set up a big motel on the Coast about a hundred and seven miles north for tired travelers of both sexes. He's got a couple of hundred girls lined up."

134

"Well get the details Chester. Fernando's the type I'll back any day of the week. But now I want you to find out what happened to the body of Grant the Roughah butler who died of a heart attack just after Rufus got it because we're going to need that body too. What about Rufus now?"

"No news boss."

"Last thing, make a rendezvous usual time with old Nick Tsvkzov. Tell him I've got something really hot for him."

"Right boss."

I hang up and go through a couple of bananas and let the peels flap a little before letting them go, they make a nice little *slappety-slap* against the windowpane. Then all of a sudden there's a wail of a siren behind me and I adjust the rearview to see what's going on and discover a state trooper in a big black and white Mercury about three feet from my rear with red and blue lights flashing. Quickly I scoot over to the slow lane thinking he wants past to get to some twenty-car spectacular up the road a ways but damn if he doesn't hit the slow lane too and with not an off-ramp in sight and so I get the general idea I'm supposed to stop, which is pretty ridiculous. I thought they gave all newborn state troopers a special course in my license numbers but I guess this one must have played hookey and since you never know when these jokers will take a notion to unload their guns at Mr. Average Motorist, I decide the best is to stop and have a talk, so I put

135

my foot down on the brake and take it easy coming to a stop because of all the shudders and whamming up front in the front end.

He pulls up behind me on the shoulder and climbs out of his Mercury like somebody's smeared the seat with honey and hitches up his pants loaded with ammo and scratches his crotch and waddles over to my door and says, "Going pretty fast in an old clunker like this, aren't you Pops?" Then he sticks his whole goddamn garlic-flavored head including cap and dark glasses in the window and says, "And you ought to know by now that there's a law against littering." He reaches in his shirt pocket and pulls out one of my banana peels and throws it plop in my lap.

For me that's about the last straw which means I'm really going to give this yokel enough rope to hang himself by both ends.

"I have half a mind," he goes on, "to make you get out and go pick up by hand every banana peel you've thrown out for the last three miles."

"Well!" I say.

"On hands and knees."

That's pretty abusive and I think this is one trooper who's going to retire at an early age on about ten bucks a week and since he's going to pay in the end I let him have his fun. He pulls out a super deluxe size traffic citation book and starts all the thumb licking and ball-point pen clicking the real dumb ones do.

"You know Pops I also noticed you didn't put on your

directional signal while changing lanes and your stoplights don't work. And I don't see any state inspection
sticker either. And it looks to me like both your windshield wipers have fallen off up there. You know, when I
think about it a little, I think I would be doing a real
service to the motoring public if I got you and this heap
of a car off the roads entirely for about as long as I can
make it stick, which is a long, long time."

Well I figure things are about to the point of going too
far so I reach for the door handle and give it a yank to get
out and the damn thing comes off in my hand. I toss it on
the floor and reach outside for that handle and get out to
face the world's most inflated state trooper.

"Know who I am?" I ask.

"No."

He chooses that moment to clear his throat right onto
my front hubcap, the unsanitary slob.

"Does that license number look at all familiar?" I ask.

He leans back and looks at the front license plate.

"Nope, sorry," he says.

I wonder what his I.Q. is. "Look," I say. "It's me,
GASCOYNE."

"Prove it," he says but I can tell he knows and has
known all the damn while.

I whip out my driver's license and flick it to him. He
glances at it and hands it back.

"So you're GASCOYNE," he says like it doesn't make any
difference at all.

"That's right. I'm GASCOYNE."

"All right GASCOYNE."

Just the same the idiot opens his citation book and starts writing.

"What the hell are you doing?" I ask, mighty peeved.

Well he sort of goes huff and puff I'll blow your house down and starts shouting at the top of his lungs, "What the hell do you think I'm doing? I'm giving you citations for speeding twenty miles over the legal limit, littering on five separate occasions, changing lanes without signaling, driving a car without stoplights, windshield wipers and a state inspection sticker, speaking with insufficient respect to a state officer of the law, and I'm going to recommend that this pile of junk be declared a menace to the motoring public and be banned from the public thoroughfares!"

All this shouting about turns his face blue and in turn I'm almost ready to pull out my big guns and vaporize this toad but I decide not to because it's pretty clear, clear as glass, that he's just following orders and I'd better save my energy for the ones who are giving them.

He tears out the ticket and I obligingly take it and make it into shredded paper that flies away in the wind.

"That's on there too," he says, "in advance."

"What?"

"Destroying state property and littering the public right-of-way a sixth time. They said you'd do it."

Well that's just too damned much to take so I step back into the car and blast off without signaling and dial Chester as fast as the old dial allows.

"Chester where the hell's O'Mallollolly now?"

"Not sure boss."

"What do you mean not sure? You're being paid to know these things Chester and you'd better get smart damn quick."

"Sure boss but I can't help it. We never heard from Gifford again and when I sent out Willy I never heard from him either. I mean I can send twenty people after O'Mallollolly but—"

"Okay Chester then you just tell me where you *think* he is right now."

"I'd guess Police Tower. What's the matter boss?"

"A state trooper stopped me for speeding."

"Holy shit!"

"Yeah," I say, "and this is going to stop right now before it really gets started. I'm going down to Police Tower right now and I want you to have Gilman and Gary and Albert waiting at the corner of Ninth and Broadway in ten minutes, got it?"

"Yeah boss but—"

"But *what* Chester?"

"Well just that why not wait for the election?"

"Drive the speed limits for three months, are you out of your mind Chester? No, O'Mallollolly's on his way out starting right now, I've let him have a free hand till now but what has he done with it but try to bite the gift horse? No siree, *out!*"

*

Gascoyne

I hang up about where the Skyway goes up in the air and where you can first see Police Tower downtown and where I'm going to make sure all hell breaks loose. I roll down the window and throw out all the rest of the goddamn bananas which makes me feel a little better, calm enough that I can think some. The trouble with characters like O'Mallollolly is you never know what they're like until you get them in and I've known the bastard for a hell of a long time. I could see this coming after the election but I figured it was best to let him go as long as he kept out of my way and then dump him the next election with a minimum of fuss, but now it looks like he wants a big fuss and that's what he's going to get. Why just now that doesn't make much sense except that his big head is like a ripe tomato and maybe this is the moment it goes rotten. He's one of those guys who just doesn't exist if he doesn't feel important and he must have decided he wasn't feeling important enough. But how the fool could forget the Scandal of '59 is beyond me. Short memory, these guys with big heads.

I turn off the Skyway onto the Infracity Expressway doing about ninety and about lose my uppers when I glance at the rearview and see a little blue Porsche right on my tail and after a moment I make out about four people inside it and then the license number which I can't believe my own eyes is the same as the silver Porsche I totaled not too many hours ago. What the hell is going on around here? Either somebody's got an angle I don't know about or I've got problems.

I pump the brakes and pull the Kaiser right into the slow lane with the Porsche sitting right on my tail like I was pulling it, and I brake some more and shoot her down the Broadway off-ramp at Seventh Street. Gary and Albert are waiting on the corner like they're supposed to be.

"Hop in back," I say. "Where the hell's Gilman?"

"Don't know boss."

"That door doesn't work," I say to Gary who's near to busting a gut trying to get in the left rear door, "use the other one."

"What's all this about boss?" Gary asks.

"Just a little talk with O'Mallollolly, that's all."

In a second Gilman hops around the corner and spots the car and climbs in the front seat. I shove her into drive and she coughs and misses a couple of times and off we go and in the rearview I can see the blue Porsche pulling out of a parking space it ducked into when I stopped. I run down Seventh Street and catch the green arrow onto the Infracity on-ramp but just in the nick of time because the Porsche hits it red but runs through anyway. I floor it up the on-ramp with the supercharger on but with the extra load in the car she's a little sluggish and so I'm only doing sixty when I merge left between two school buses burning up our tax money and it looks like seventy's about tops as I work my way over to the third lane and decide to keep on that one.

O'Mallollolly's probably got his telescope trained on us right now from Police Tower and I fiddle with the rearview which always jiggles out of place and spot the

141

Porsche behind, second lane, and something else moving up fast, lanes three and four, and in a minute I can see it's a very even formation of six black and white state trooper cars which glide past the Porsche and come right up to my rear and sit there. O'Mallollolly's getting the big guns out all right though he's sure forgot to check with the owner first. I don't say anything to the boys about what's behind because I can see that Albert is already getting a little stiff.

There's a funny thing about this Kaiser I own which is it behaves fine if it's just me inside but with anybody else all sorts of things start happening for no goddamn reason at all. Well old Gilman is sitting there in the front seat beside me minding his own business with that sort of freeway glaze over his eyes when *bang* the glove compartment door pops open and my jar of Micro-Mice rolls out right into his lap. He sort of stares at it like it was a knife in his stomach and then groans a little and picks up the jar and looks inside. "*Mice!*" he screams and starts rolling down the window. I lean over and grab the jar away and put it back into the glove compartment which causes me to lose control of the car and ends up that I pull the thing so far right that I cross both right lanes and go up on the shoulder and blow into kindling wood one of those No Stopping signs, but by that time I'm back into control and soon get the thing running in a straight line again in the right direction.

Gilman puts his feet up on the glove compartment door to keep that from happening again but I can see old Albert in the back is in trouble trying to roll down the window which like the door it's in doesn't work. "Use the other one," I say and Gary catches on and rolls down his window and Albert vomits out that side and fortunately for us not inside the car, but I imagine the rear quarter panel is a big mess.

Just then Marge calls.

"Hi Marge."

"Hello dear, say, I'm still being followed."

"Don't worry about it Marge, it happens every day. Where are you now?"

"Having lunch at the FAT PHEASANT AND OLD GREYHOUND GRILL AND RESTAURANT overlooking Lake Lobotomples," she says.

"Jesus Christ do you know what things cost there Marge? About five times what they are anywhere else around there," I say and I know what I'm talking about since I own the joint.

"I know dear but the chairs are soft and the view nice and the music is relaxing—"

"Look Marge take my advice right this minute and get out of that clip joint and run down the road about a mile to a little place made out of an old trolley and called STEVIE'S SENSATIONAL SANDWICHES where you can really eat well for nothing, pay a dollar and you come out of there absolutely bloated."

"Bloated? Well dear I don't think I really want to get bloated, you know, just a *bite* to eat."

"It'll cost you five bucks just to look at a glass of water,

I swear. I mean look Marge you're up there on a business trip and not a pleasure cruise and if you want to live high off the hog why do it on your own time."

"Dear. You say this is a business trip," she says.

"That's right."

"Well what am I supposed to get out of it?"

"Hell Marge all I can say is you ought to be grateful since you're getting a free tour of Mt. Pastiche National Forest and it's not costing you a damn cent."

"Well dear that's all very nice. Mt. Pastiche National Forest *is* a beautiful place. I love it. I love the trees. I love the mountains. I love—"

"Calm down Marge."

"Shut up. I love the lakes. That's why I have come up here about five times a year for the last ten years. And that's why a free tour of the place is a really new and exciting experience. I expect to throw myself in the lake with joy any moment now."

"Finished?"

"Yes," and then she goes and hangs up.

Damn that woman I say to myself, she'll be calling me up and asking me to send up a Brink's armored car with sacks of silver dollars next thing. She'll have us all on the streets pretty soon the way she's going. I'll bet she unloads fifteen bucks in the FAT PHEASANT.

But damn, all this distracts me from what's at hand and I find myself in the third lane when I ought to be in the far right because the Police Tower off-ramp is coming up damn fast so I scoot over right and everybody behind me

144

starts edging over to the slow lane and I brake and roll down the off-ramp and go right onto Water Boulevard and then left a block later onto Avenue of Police Commissioner O'Mallollolly and run up that to Police Tower and bounce into the executive parking lot. I roll slowly past the nine black 1965 limousines and turn toward my parking slot near the side entrance. I pull up to it but damn if there isn't some shriveled-up old fart crouching down digging out my brass nameplate with a hammer and chisel. I let a short one out of the air horn and then force him out of the way completely by running the Kaiser right up against the wall so he can't get at the nameplate at all.

We climb out of the car and I recognize the old man who's dressed in overalls as former Police Commissioner MacWigo, 1955-59, who I got out with the famous Scandal of '59. Nice that somebody found something for him to do around the old place though I can't exactly approve of this particular odd job he's got.

"Your time has come GASCOYNE," he says.

"My time will come when I decide."

"They all say that, they all say that."

"My time will come when I decide."

Obviously we don't see eye-to-eye on this matter so I give the sign to the boys and we start heading for the side entrance. Across the Avenue the six troopers' cars have pulled up to the curb and all the troopers are standing on the sidewalk looking across at us, must be about thirty of them, and some are watching us through field glasses. I

145

sort of suspect O'Mallollolly has told them to stand by conspicuously as a show of force but I think they're really standing there waiting for the air to be cleared so they'll know which side to jump to when jumping time comes.

Just then the plate glass of the side entrance door goes *crash* and tinkles to the ground and three submachine-gun barrels stick out and wave around. "Drop boys," I say and all of us fall down behind the big granite boulders of the Japanese garden God-knows-who decided to put there, damn good idea from our point of view.

"All right GASCOYNE what do you want?" calls out some ignoramus.

"In," I say.

"What?"

"In!"

"Goddamn speak up GASCOYNE."

"*In!* I-N!"

Then I hear whispers inside the entrance saying, "He wants in he said."

"Why?" another voice calls out.

"None of your goddamn business," I say.

"You've got to tell us why," somebody else inside says.

Then there are more whispers and I throw one of those little white garden pebbles at Gary and hit him on the head. He gives out a little scream but after awhile turns his head at me.

"*Psst!*" I say. "In exactly thirty seconds we all open fire on the door."

"Ok—" he chokes, "okay boss."

146

Gary whispers to Albert and Albert to Gilman.

The thirty seconds whip by pretty fast, I guess, since I don't have a watch and I don't think anybody else does either, and then me and Gary start pumping lead into the doorway. Gilman joins in but then Albert the ass faints. We keep on blasting away anyway until it looks like they've retreated from the entrance completely. I take a chance and stand up and of course nobody shoots at me. I can see over the parking lot and across the street the troopers are all laying down behind their cars.

"Come on boys, charge!" I say and while Gilman picks up Albert and throws him over his back Gary and I move in on the entrance door and find the entrance and hallway and executive elevator completely abandoned by the defenders so we move in and take over. There's a hell of a racket coming from upstairs however and I'm a little bit afraid of a counteroffensive or a trap or something, especially the way the executive elevator is sitting there, doors wide open and all ready and waiting.

"I suspect this is a trap," I say. "We'd better take the fire escape up."

"Anything you say boss."

We duck Albert's head under the cold-water fountain and before we leave I reach in the elevator and push fifteen so they'll think we're coming up. The door snaps closed and up she goes.

"Follow me," I command and we go through a little door opposite the elevator and down into the boiler room and cross that and come out the other side of the building where the interior fire escape is. The thing's rarely used because the doors are one-way in a way that if you go out you can't get back in the building except through the executive suite fire escape door which has an external lock to which only I have the key. Just the same we listen a few minutes at the foot of the stairs for unusual sounds but hear nothing and so start up. About now, I'm thinking, the elevator ought to be up top and they'll be wondering how we're coming up, but all right since they're probably thinking I'm working my way up one of the three main staircases, which I could do easily enough except that I like the element of surprise. I've got a hell of a lot of friends in this joint which O'Mallollolly is going to discover pretty soon if he doesn't know it now though I will admit he's probably got the whole top floor except for the Goon Squad in his pocket, but there's a lot of country between there and the ground.

The hike up the stairs is so exhausting we have to stop at the third-floor landing to catch our breath for about five minutes and I'm thinking maybe we ought to try to force open one of the fire escape doors and commandeer a service elevator. I'm not used to this sort of exercise though I've been getting a lot of it these last days, still it seems to be harder rather than easier, and at the rate we're going it'll take us two hours to get to the fifteenth floor.

Still I decide it's worth a little more of a try so we hike up to the fifth floor and by putting our ears against the door we gather there's a big commotion going on inside

and after we're well enough rested we stand back and
start blasting away at the hinges, metal flying all over the
place. Gilman's revolver all of a sudden falls apart into
about seven pieces but since Albert's sitting down not
being able to take the noise and trying to swallow an aspirin without water, Gilman borrows his.

We blast away some more and pretty soon the door
collapses and I shout "Charge!" and we charge in, and
what a mess is there. Desks and filing cabinets are over-
turned all over the place and cops and secretaries are
taking potshots at each other from behind them and all
sorts of stuff is flying through the air like lamps and small
office machines and bundles of paper. But because the
racket's so bad and we come in at the end of a hallway
nobody really notices us and all we've got to do is pass
through two office doors to get to an elevator. We get
down on hands and knees and crawl along the hall a few
feet to an office door and pop in there where we find our-
selves without much choice confronting a heavily armed
group momentarily engaged in lining up metal office
chairs with foam rubber seats and setting the seats on fire
and rolling them flaming across the hall into an apparently enemy office. I approach the guy I take it is in
charge and who I've seen before but never met and I'm
not sure if he knows who I am, perhaps to my advantage.

"What's the situation?" I ask.

"Well," he says, "the O'Mallollolly forces seem to be
getting the upper hand. At the moment they control an
expanding pie-shaped sector that includes Birth and

Death Certificates, Payroll, both lavatories and the janitor's closet, also a small strategically located enclave in the snack bar kitchen. But there's an element of uncertainty here which is that the expanding O'Mallollolly forces seem to be broken into several factions."

"Hmm."

"But even all this is in doubt because we've heard rumors about GASCOYNE water reinforcements from the sixth floor."

"I see. Who controls the elevators?"

"As far as I know at the moment," he says, "a small independent group from Parking Meters, third floor, that's gone completely mercenary."

"Thanks pal," I say and we work our way through the office to the other cross-corridor and when we get there all we have to do is turn right and go a few steps, must be a truce area because things are pretty calm. I push the Up button and watch the numbers light up as the elevator comes down from the seventh floor. The doors open and the thing's filled with about five guys with submachine guns looking pretty businesslike.

"Fourteen please," I say, pulling Gary and Gilman and Albert in behind me. They're a little timid about this crowd I can tell.

"What's it worth to you, the fourteenth floor?" the guy at the controls asks as he closes the door.

"Not a damn cent, just get this thing going," I say.

"Who the hell do you think you are?" the joker asks.

"GASCOYNE," I say.

He looks me over and pushes the fourteen button and up we go, that's the sort of respect I like accorded to my name, which is as good as hard cash in most situations. We hit floor fourteen and out we go and things are quiet up here like on a normal day, except that just peeking in one office I can see everybody's either on the telephone or helping move desks and filing cabinets into barricades. We slip out the fire escape without any trouble and climb the stairs to fifteen where I unlock the executive fire escape door and we push our way into the executive bedroom, nobody else there.

We cross over to the door leading to O'Mallollolly's office and I figure the best thing to do is just walk in, no gunplay unless necessary, and that's what we do except for Albert who goes and passes out again. O'Mallollolly's sitting at his desk reading a list into the phone and surrounded by the Goon Squad and when we come in he just keeps on reading.

". . . O'Brian, total demotion. Rogers, dismissal without compensation or benefits. Black, dismissal with half pension. Scoville, transfer to State Forestry Service. Jones, Arthur, dismissal with public trial for appropriating municipal property. MacGanymede, demotion from subcommissioner to third-floor janitor or dismissal, at his option."

Those are all my people he's canning of course and it's putting it pretty mildly to say he's doing it without my permission. I suspect he's bought out the rest like the Goon Squad which, by the way Victor refuses to look at me in the eye, I can tell I'll have to write off, but what I

151

want to know is where O'Mallollolly's getting the backing for this kind of operation which isn't cheap and isn't something he can pull all by himself.

He hangs up the phone and right away starts dialing another number which really pisses me off. Here I am standing here right in front of him with not exactly a birthday party expression on my face, though I've never seen him look as hot and bothered as he does now. I decide I might as well pull out the big gun right now.

"All right O'Mallollolly," I say, "I want your resignation. Three copies, signed and witnessed."

He clamps the phone between his shoulder and cheek and starts chewing on a fingernail and says, "You're through GASCOYNE, go away."

Just then the door opens and O'Mallollolly just about falls off his chair but it's only some sergeant who comes in and plops a paper down on the desk and runs right out. O'Mallollolly looks at it and it's the first time I've ever seen him sweat between the nose and upper lip and I think maybe he's just suffered a big defeat on the fifth floor.

"I'm not through," I say, "I've just begun and I want all nine subcommissioners out and replaced by MacGanymede who's going to take your place until the election."

He doesn't seem to be listening when I say that and hangs up the phone and dials again and I'm wondering what the hell I have to do to get it through his thick skull that he's at the end of the line.

"Listen O'Mallollolly—"

"Shut up GASCOYNE, and go away will you?"

"You know who you're talking to don't you," I say pretty mad, "you know who you're talking to. Me, GASCOYNE."

"Yeah, and I've got better ways to spend my time."

"You do, do you? Well look O'Mallollolly either you start scribbling out a resignation right this minute or I'm going to throw a scandal at you and Police Tower so big they'll be talking about it in Medicine Bow Wyoming for ten years. I'll make it easy for you the first way but—"

"Big deal."

"You interrupted me," I say.

"Because I'm busy and it's my turn. GASCOYNE I want you out of this building in twenty minutes, out of town in twenty-eight hours, out of the state in thirty-one hours. I've written it down in case you forget."

He searches through about five piles of papers on his desk and comes up with a little scrap of envelope and hands it to me with the figures on, I guess, but I can't read a thing up close without my glasses.

Just then the phone rings and O'Mallollolly picks it up and listens a moment and hangs up and says to Victor behind him, "Start moving the desks over there against the door and throw up a barricade out in the reception office and don't let anybody in here without a signed pass, got it?"

The Goon Squad starts moving across the office but rather reluctantly because they're supposed to be exempted from manual labor and O'Mallollolly gives them a dirty look and gets back on the phone leaving me stand there like a goddamn hatrack.

"Look O'Mallollolly—"

"Hey I'm busy, huh? Scram, before I have to throw you out."

Well things are going pretty far and I figure the best way to handle this is on my own territory where at least I'll get the respect I'm entitled to and be able to fix O'Mallollolly's wagon in a way nobody'll be able to repair.

"Well I guess we ought to get a start on it," I say to the boys and we head out around the furniture the Goon Squad's piling up, sweating and swearing like the devil at the way their white uniforms are getting all smudged up, serves them right. We climb over the pile of sofas and coffee tables in the reception room and walk to the executive elevator which is waiting there ready and open and I push the button.

Down we go but I change my mind and hit the five button because I want to see how things are going on there which has always been one of my best strongholds when things get difficult. The elevator stops and the doors fly open and I can't see a damn thing because the place is filled with smoke and what smells like tear gas with small arms and machine guns going off everywhere in little orange flashes and everybody shouting their heads off and glass breaking and furniture clanging. Just then a breeze carries away some of the smoke in front of the elevator and I can just make out three cops setting up a small mortar and then this officer comes running past, black all over his face, and sees me and runs up and cries "GASCOYNE!" He takes my hand and I'm pretty moved by this and so I take out my monogrammed handkerchief which unfortunately isn't clean but he'll never notice in this mess and I give it to him and say, "God bless you child!"

"Oh GASCOYNE thank you!" he says and rushes away tying the handkerchief around the tip of one of those poles they use for opening transoms and high windows, and he disappears into the smoke chanting a very flattering version of "Onward Christian Soldiers."

All of a sudden there are a couple of shouts close by and somebody yells "Retreat! All is lost!" and a crowd of cops and secretaries emerges out of the fog toward us and a corporal shouts, "GASCOYNE, help! Save us!"

Well there are just too goddamn many to fit into the elevator so I very reluctantly press the one button and the doors close and down we go to the ground floor where I remember we've forgotten poor Albert, passed out in the executive bedroom, but what the hell it was his fault. The elevator doors open upon a pretty thick crowd of officers and policemen and secretaries and office help who are carrying guns and broken furniture legs as clubs and looking quite excited, but everybody goes quiet when I step out of the elevator with Gilman and Gary following. The crowd silently parts and lets us pass through the side entrance and I can hear people whispering, "It's GASCOYNE." Though this is all rather touching I'm a bit bothered by the feeling that this isn't really my territory and that O'Mallollolly is damn close to having all of Police Tower to himself, which isn't good.

As we walk through the crowd to the car a party of wounded stops to let us pass and I look down at the stretcher to see ex-Subcommissioner MacGanymede lying flat on his back. He looks up at me dimly and as blood oozes from his lips he says, "I tried, GASCOYNE, I tried. I only wish . . ." But the cold hand of death stops what promised to be memorable last words. Poor MacGanymede, a good man, hate to lose him.

Slowly we work our way through the pressing and staring crowd whose hostility is held back by the awesome spectacle. I see here and there a club raised to strike but always there is another hand that reaches up gently and pulls it down which almost makes me weep. We reach the Kaiser and some brave soul jumps forward to open the front door for me and helps me inside while Gary the ass tries to get in the left back door. "Use the other door for God's sake," I say and he runs around to the other side and Gilman gets in the front.

I press the starter button but I'll be damned if the lousy thing won't start. *Wow-a-wow-a-wow-a* goes the starter without a sign of the motor catching, probably the starter pinion's jammed which happens now and then.

"Say," I call out the window to the fellow who opened the door, "do you suppose you could give us a little push?"

The fellow looks around and says something and then

as if by magic the whole crowd converges on the rear of the Kaiser and starts pushing with some even fighting for pushing room and some even go around the front to pull. This is all so overwhelmingly moving I can hardly see straight enough to drop the thing in low, and we get pushed onto Avenue of Police Commissioner O'Mallollolly and then they really push and soon we're rolling fast enough to turn over the automatic transmission and motor, and the thing catches and coughs and off we go in a cloud of exhaust.

I turn left onto Tenth Avenue and dump Gilman and Gary off at the corner of Water Boulevard and head on for the Infracity on-ramp pretty tired out by the Police Tower exercise and wanting to stop and take ten winks, but I haven't got the time the way things are going. What gives me the headache is trying to figure out why O'Mallollolly is going to all the effort to take over Police Tower in his nasty way when he knows he's cutting his own throat and public life-span down to three months at the most. Against me he hasn't got a chance and it's almost as if he actually wants me to wipe him off the face of the map which smells pretty fishy. Well, I decide, I'm the one who chooses the time and place around here so I'm going to wait a little to see if something's brewing I don't see and which makes a little more sense. And then there are a hell of a lot of other things to get cleared up.

I swing left onto the Infracity on-ramp and hit the supercharger and am glad to see the old Kaiser's got back some of its poop, and I sail very nicely into the slow lane and then squeeze through the mess to the fast lane and run it up to seventy-five, not wanting to push it too much. Then I give Chester a ring.

"Yeah boss. Got a report from Fitz in Police Tower. Sorry."

"We may have lost a battle Chester, but the war's just begun. What else is new?"

"We got Grant the butler's body from the Phoenix Crematorium just in the nick of time. Called Tsvkzov, he'll meet you at the usual time and wants you to be in seat thirty-eight."

"Good," I say.

"Now as for Fernando, he doesn't need any more financing, he says."

"Doesn't *need* any more?" I say.

"That's what he said boss."

"Hell what's got into him? I've always backed him from the very start and he always comes to me before anybody else. Suddenly getting choosey, isn't he?"

"Don't know boss. Maybe he's waiting for the O'Mallollolly thing to blow over."

"Shit! Chester you call Fernando. If he won't do business with me now and damn quick he'll find it so rough he'll have to go out of town to take a goddamn leak, damn!"

"Now wait a minute boss, I wouldn't lose your head over—"

"Chester I don't lose my head, are you ever going to understand?"

"Sorry boss. All I wanted to say—"

"Be quick about it."

"All I want to say is that maybe Fernando's been out of town so long he doesn't know what's going on," he says.

"Well he's going to find out right now. Call him."

"Now really boss why don't—"

"Shut your mouth Chester and get on that phone and give him hell, understand?"

I hang up damned pissed off. The trouble with Chester is he's got a weak spine and is no good at carrying out orders when they don't strike his fancy like moments like this, though I've got to put up with it because he's the best of the whole shooting match and even with his bad points it would take me months to replace him with all the training a position like this calls for. He was a natural, I thought, with his pretty good telephone voice and manner which is what I hired him for seven years ago, by phone as a matter of fact, and one of these days I'll have to hop down to GASCOYNE CENTER to see what the guy looks like because I don't think I ever saw his written application or picture, that's what I pay other people to shuffle papers for. Chester hasn't got an easy job I know but this is no time to bitch about it and somebody's got to do it since I work this way of going through Chester for the simple reason that people respect more what they can't see. Most of these guys I've backed and run like

159

Louis and Fernando and Mark I've never seen or talked
to over the phone and Chester told me it took Mark six
months to believe I really existed which is the way things
ought to be. This O'Mallollolly thing shows you what
happens when you don't make people keep their distance.
They get ideas and they're always the wrong ones.

The SLEEPY DELL EXECUTIVE GARDEN ESTATES off-
ramp pops up and I merge right and pump the brakes and
bring her down the off-ramp and notice just as I'm turning the corner at the bottom that things are getting a little
crowded behind because the blue Porsche is back on my
tail and behind it what looks like two plainclothes police
Thunderbirds. I whip through the orange light at the underpass but the red doesn't stop them and they all come
right on through really messing up the traffic situation. I
decide that if the chance comes I'll throw them off but no
rush since where I'm going at the moment is no big secret,
no sense pushing it and I'm a little in a hurry right now.
O'Mallollolly's probably just trying to throw his weight
around but is too scared to really do anything and I probably know the guys in the T-birds anyway.

I roll down Vieworama Ridge Drive at about forty-five
and turn right onto Mirindaranda Road and head for the
Widow Roughah's joint. Just then the phone rings.

"GASCOYNE?" some voice asks.

"Yeah, who else? Who the hell's this?" I ask.

"Never mind. We're going to give you a chance to make
a deal."

"Who the hell's we?" I ask again.

"Never mind. Are you interested in a deal?"

"For what?"

"To make it easier for both of us. To ease you nice and soft out of the tree you've got yourself up," he says.

"I'm up no tree I know of."

"We'll tell you which tree you're up if you want to make a deal."

"Look mister," I say, "you've got the funniest ideas of the way things are in this town of anyone I know," and I hang up. This sort of thing happens often enough, some little frog looks at the pond and decides it's worth making a splash in, they've seen too many westerns. Or probably some crackpot trying to make a little off my tiff with O'Mallollolly.

I go straight at the Mirindaranda split and get to the Roughah main gate and decide to go on in, so I snake the Kaiser up the white gravel drive and nose it into my parking slot and am pretty pissed off to see that some joker has swiped my nameplate, two in one day makes a man feel a little unwanted. I reach out and pull the door open from the outside and climb out and crunch around to the front of the house and give the door a good beating. After a couple of minutes with my feet going numb, the Widow Roughah still dressed in that slinky black gown of hers opens the door and lets me in.

"All right Nade," I demand, "who swiped my name-plate?"

"Don't call me Nade. Nadine. N-a-d-i-n-e."

"Look Nade, you tell me who swiped my nameplate and I'll call you Nadine."

She looks at me with those two ramrod eyes of coal black and says, "I swiped it."

"What did you do a silly thing like that for?"

She sort of goes soft and drops herself down in a big white polarbearskin Morris chair.

"Well?" I ask.

"You ask too many questions, GASCOYNE, I can't stand it I tell you, I can't stand it!"

Very casually I pull out my automatic and slip on the silencer and screw off the safety and pick a large expanse of blank wall and start blasting away but since my aim isn't as good as it used to be the G comes out looking like a C and I can't seem to get the top on the A and the S is a real mess and I just get started on the C when I run completely out of ammo.

"Just to show you Nade my nameplate is not to be tampered with," I say as I pour a little water out of a flower vase over the barrel of my gun which is quite hot.

"Shall we move to the sitting room?" she asks, stretching and getting up. "The smoke gets in my eyes here."

She's right about that one so we make our way to the sitting room which is a small affair done in red velvet and that sort of stuff with a pitch-black ceiling and a black wall-to-wall carpet. She sits down on a little chair and pulls out a pair of dark glasses and puts them on.

"All right," she says, "what's to be done for Jeremy Armstrong?"

"Well according to my doctor friend the only thing to do is give his old octopus arm an hourly rinse with a strong solution of BONANZA BANQUETTE ALL-PURPOSE MARVELOUS DETERGENT WITH FORMULA SUD 39."

"Oh," she says. "I guess I'd better tell him then."

"All right," I say and she goes out another door and I think this is as good a chance as I'll have for awhile to snooze so I plunk myself down on a couch tired as hell and no sooner do I get myself stretched out than there she is back again with Jeremy Armstrong in tow. I sit back up.

"Mr. GASCOYNE how can I thank you?"

Well I don't know what he has to thank me for because he's still got his tentacle hanging out and at the moment toying with his button-down collar. In fact I think the thing actually looks a little longer and fatter.

"Well son," I say, "there are a lot of ways but let's make sure this soap thing works before we worry about anything else."

"Yes sir. I'm sure it will."

"Now don't get your hopes up too high."

"Oh no," he says just as the old tentacle gets tired of the button and starts swinging around so much it goes *splat* right against the wall making Armstrong stagger a little. "It's just that when you come back from the wars," he goes on with some difficulty, "people never seem to understand."

163

Gascoyne

"Well I understand," I say.

Just then the tentacle goes into its feeding position and Armstrong gives it a half-peanut with jerky little movements.

"Yes I know," he says. "I mean it's not my fault. But I shouldn't talk about it like this. Well fine weather we've had today and say Mr. GASCOYNE Nadine's told me a lot about you but I'm afraid I never did catch your profession. What—"

Well at this moment the tentacle chooses to curl up and go to sleep leaving Armstrong high and dry, and his eyes roll up and his knees go soft and he crumples down on the floor. Nadine runs over to the door and shouts for somebody and in a second a real bitchy-looking nurse marches in and grabs Armstrong by the foot and drags him out. Good riddance because I can't spend any more time worrying about the poor bastard, I've got enough problems of my own.

Nadine goes and sits back down on her little chair.

"All right," she says, "I'm going to talk."

"About what?"

"Talk, sing, spill the beans, let the cat out of the bag, 'fess up."

"You don't say," I say.

"Yes," she says.

"Why at this particular moment?" I ask.

"Well GASCOYNE I've got to do it sooner or later."

"That's true."

164

There's a pretty awkward silence and then I ask, "Well why did you swipe my nameplate?"

"I can tell you anything but that," she says going stiff and hysterical. "But let me confess now."

"Well wait a minute Nade, let's not be in such a big hurry. We've got to be sensible about this sort of thing."

"I guess you're right GASCOYNE but sometimes it's so hard."

"You've got to try."

"I know," she says softly.

She pulls out a handkerchief but doesn't do anything with it and then she gets up and starts pacing back and forth on the pitch-black carpet.

"I was born—" she moans but I put a stop to that.

"Oh stop it Nade, you can't do it like that and you know it."

"But I can't help it."

"Just answer my questions."

"But the trouble is GASCOYNE when you do it that way you ask all the important ones first and those are the ones I don't want to answer until last."

"Damn, all right," I say, "but I'm in a hurry, I've got an appointment. Where were you born?"

"Damn you cruel beast," she says bursting into tears and stomping her feet, "all you want to do is dig out dirty underwear and wave it around, monster!"

"That's right Nade, I'm just a good old-fashioned villain who straps helpless girls to the railroad tracks."

"That's exactly what you are you filthy slob!"

She grabs a Chinese vase and heaves it at my head but I duck and it goes through a mirror. Then I get up and give her a couple of slaps across the face and twist her arm and throw her down on the couch where she whines deep behind her cat's teeth and tries to bite and kick me.

"Sit still or I'll start breaking things," I say.

She lets out with a sort of convulsion and then goes limp, sweating.

"All right that's better. Where were you born?"

"In America."

She spits in my eye. I soften her up with a few more slaps.

"Where in America?"

"I can't tell."

I twist her arm.

"*Ohio!*" she gasps.

"Where in Ohio?" I ask with more twisting.

"San—"

"Yes?"

"*Eee!* Sandusky."

I relax the pressure.

"Jesus you're good GASCOYNE," she sighs.

"Not so bad yourself Nade."

"Mmm. That feels good."

"We must get on. What was O'Mallollolly doing here the afternoon of the murder before the murder or during it as the case may be?"

"I won't tell," she says and holds her breath and turns red and then a little bluish.

I give her a tap on the stomach.

"*Pou-ak!*" she explodes. "How dare you touch me there you dirty old man!"

She gets her teeth in my hand and chomps down real hard. With no little pain I free my hand and look at the row of fresh tooth marks with the feeling that I've seen somewhere else an identical row of fresh tooth marks on someone else's hand very recently but I can't remember who or where.

I slap her a couple of times and her nose starts bleeding.

"Talk goddamn you or I'll ring your neck!"

"All right," she says with a swallow, her eyes gone glassy. "Would you mind repeating the question?"

"Ah, something about O'Mallollolly being here the afternoon of the murder."

"Yes of course he was, I told you that."

"Yes, but why?"

She sobs. "To conceal evidence."

"What evidence?"

"The murder weapon."

"Yes, go on, try to speak in complete sentences if you possibly can."

"The murder weapon. He gave it to me to hide."

"Where did you hide it?"

"Well," she says, "now that's a little personal."

"All right skip that. Where is it now?"

"In that desk drawer."

"That one?" I say, pointing at a desk in the corner.

She bites her lip and says, "Yes!"

I spring up and go over to the desk and pull open the drawer and sure enough there's the murder weapon but sure enough too there's something traveling fast toward the back of my head and I duck just in time to miss a genuine meat cleaver, wherever she pulled that one from, which sinks three inches into the wall back of where my head was.

"Did you throw that?" I ask.

But she's about ready to launch a magazine stand at me so I pick up the desk chair and knock her out cold. Then I pick her up and toss her back down on the couch and pat her cheeks to make her come to.

"Oh where am I?"

"Right where you started from, only now with a little sense knocked into you."

"Crummy bastard you'd strike your own mother."

"Have already on more than one occasion."

She starts screaming and whimpering so I have to put my hand over her mouth and she tries to bite my fingers so I've got to soften her up a little more.

"All right, I'll talk!" she gasps, tears springing from her eyes. "What was the question?"

"I haven't asked it yet."

"Perverted sadist for beating me up for nothing."

"All wrong. Hand over that insurance policy!"

168

"Over my dead body!"

"Is that a request?"

She slips a long-fingernailed hand free and jabs me right there which has the effect of causing much pain and throwing me off balance and off the couch and down on the floor flat on my back. She stands up on the couch and jumps off with her three-inch spikes aimed squarely at my exposed belly.

"Die you nasty old fart!" she shrieks as she plummets downward.

Fortunately I make an agile twist away and upwards only an instant before her spikes would have speared me and she hits the floor with a tremendous crash and her spikes sink into the carpet and into the floor and she stands there uncertainly with her arms waving when all of a sudden the floor under her gives way and the carpet rips and she vanishes from sight, leaving only her rumpled black slinky gown behind, peeled off by the narrowness of the aperture.

Gingerly I test the floor and edge my way toward the hole and look down in, dark as hell it is.

"Hey Nade!" I call down. "You all right?"

No answer.

"*Psst!*" I call again. "Come on Nade cut out the horseplay. I'm in a hurry damn it."

Still no answer. This is pretty annoying so I edge away from the hole and go over to the desk and take out the murder weapon. Underneath is of all things an insurance policy and a quick peek at the large print reveals it's just the one we want. I take down the policy number and the name of the company which I can read and put the thing back in the drawer.

I pussyfoot it back to the hole and call down, "Hey Nade, I've got to go, really." No sound. "Well I'll see you later Nade. Give Chester a ring if you need anything."

I work my way back from the hole and then go out the door and notice as I pass through the living room I'm already ten minutes late according to the clock there and this could end up with a real mess.

Tired as I am from all that exertion I can't afford to slow down so I hotfoot it out the front door and into the Kaiser which fortunately starts right off though there's a knock in the engine at first I've never heard before and I wonder if maybe this one's had it. A new or reconditioned engine lasts me on the average of two months and sometimes three and I'm going on the third month now and the odometer's hitting the high ninety thousands, so at least from now on I'm getting my money's worth.

I back her up and throw her down the gravel driveway and shoot out the main gate and right off pick up the two police T-birds and the blue Porsche I scraped off coming in and we all parade down Mirindaranda Road. All three of them are not bad at the signal game which is something usually no more than two can play and I begin to think that maybe they've got a gadget in their cars to trigger the signals which is something I've been trying to get for a long time. If they do, O'Mallollolly's been putting in the overtime for a long time all right because something like this doesn't get fixed up overnight and if there's one thing I'd like to know right now it's just how long he's been playing games. Not much longer anyway, though I've got to make up my mind about the Scandal of '65, it's got to be something strong and forceful to capture the public imagination.

I turn left at Wahahneeot and hit the on-ramp to the Urban Circle Uptown Turnpike Tollroad and shoot up it and merge in between a couple of those house trailers that are so big you wonder where they ever come from and where the hell they're going and then I crank the Kaiser up to seventy and slip her into the fast lane and in a second the Thunderbirds settle down in a flight pattern in lanes three and four creating a dangerous traffic situation but that's the sort of thing they like. The Porsche seems to be hopping around the two slow lanes which means that if he can do it without piling into the back of a slow-moving truck he's pretty damn good and I'm wondering who he's working for if it isn't O'Mallollolly. Things are not running too well I must admit if somebody's following you you don't know on your own territory and you can't do much about it, but I'm learning my lesson from this sort of thing and the Police Tower battle and trouble is with the way I've got things set up now I only know about twenty of my guys by sight, more like fifteen, and most of them aren't any good during the showdown hour and so what I've got to do is set up a little private army of fifty to a hundred under some private police patrol front or something like Pinkertons. You don't need this sort of thing very often but when you do you need it bad.

About then Marge calls.

"Hi Marge. Get up to Condor's Crag yet?"

"No," she says pretty coldly.

"Well where are you then?"

"Just sitting," she says.

"Well where dear?"

"Oh I'm still at the FAT PHEASANT AND OLD GREY-HOUNDE."

"What?"

"I said I'm still at the FAT PHEASANT AND OLD—"

"I heard you," I say, "and I just want to know what the hell you're still doing there and how much this is costing me."

"Well I'm still here because eating takes time, I mean we're not all like you dear. I mean sometimes we have to stop and eat and sometimes that takes a couple of hours and sometimes we have to sleep and that cuts out a whole eight hours of each day, really awfully inefficient I admit dear, but that's the way the rest of us are made."

"Hell I don't care how you're made just as long as you don't use it as an excuse to throw money all over the landscape. If you can stay in bed eight hours every night fine and dandy, though I do think you sleep too much Marge and I sure don't see the point of spending three dollars an hour of my hard-earned money for the purpose of passing out on a flat level space with a couple of sheets and blankets and pillows around and I see the point even less of sitting in the FAT PHEASANT and paying the joint ten bucks an hour to shovel food into your mouth, you get just as much nutritional value out of a big chocolate bar that costs half a buck and takes two minutes to eat nuts and all."

"And I suppose—" she says and sort of chokes.

"What?"

"And I suppose you're going to tell me I ought to eat two chocolate bars a day and cut my sleep down to a half hour and then what do you want me to do stay up all night—"

"Calm down Marge. Look at Chester now, he's been up for three nights in a row now and he's doing just fine, even a little better than usual."

"How nice—"

"Stop screaming Marge."

"I'm not screaming, I'm raving," she says and boy she's doing both for my money. "I mean there are just so many wonderful exciting things I could do if I stayed up all night on two chocolate bars. I just love to knit. *Knit!* Just think with all that time on my hands I could knit you a car cover or me a wall-to-wall knitted carpet or a circus tent. Do you suppose I could buy a chocolate bar at the FAT PHEASANT?"

"No. STEVIE'S SENSATIONAL SANDWICHES has them."

"Whoopie!"

"Marge there's something wrong with your attitude and I wish you'd stop it."

"All right!" she shrieks.

"All right. Now what the hell did you call for?"

She doesn't say a damn thing but she hasn't hung up yet either, I'm getting pretty pissed off.

"Come off it Marge, what did you call for?"

"Oh," she says, "oh just to chew the fat. Not much else to do around all this scenery except chew the fat."

"Hell you're supposed to be on your way to Condor's Crag. What the hell's got into you woman?"

"Look mister I called to tell you that as I was walking out to that stupid car some man comes up to me and asks me to call you and ask you if you're interested in a deal of I don't know what sort but he wouldn't say anything else so I called you and what do I get but a lecture on how to live life for a dollar a day, gas and automobile repairs not included."

Then the bitch hangs up just like that.

Well I've got my own problems to worry about and one of them is the Tollroad Tollgate which is coming into view and I check the rearview again and see that nothing's changed back there with my following friends so just to give them a little jolt I snap on the supercharger and whiz her up to eighty-five and then dial the tollgate central phone.

"It's GASCOYNE here and I'm coming through number one as per usual."

"Hold on," some wise one answers, "you've got to stop and pay a toll like anybody else now GASCOYNE."

"Sorry buster too late."

174

The light stays red on number one and a couple of cops rush out and throw up one of those wooden sawhorses, the optimists, and they see me still coming and they start running away in all directions. I snap on the headlights and put on the air horn and touch off a pair of tracer bazookas I've got slung under the front of the car which go shooting through the tollgate with red and orange tracer flames though they won't blow anything up, a pretty display. Then in the last instant I catch the scene in the rearview and one of the T-birds is still on my tail while the other is pulling right to pay his toll and I can't see where the Porsche's gone, and I zoom through the gate at about ninety and blast the wooden sawhorse into splinters up in the sky to make rain with, and then when I'm clear I watch behind the T-bird shooting in toward the gate but in the last second it veers just a bit left and plows square into the little glass house where the guys stand to take the tolls. The whole affair just flies to pieces up into the air and I can see shooting up and coming down little shiny glistening specks which are the nickels and dimes and quarters Mr. Average Motorist has been shelling out all day long, high into the air like a cross between fireworks and a fountain display, but I can't see a thing of the T-bird unless it's up there floating around too.

The other one which stopped to pay its toll must not have the exact change or something because I see no sign of it, but the blue Porsche somehow made it through and it is catching up with me pretty fast, damn, and I won't be able to shake him here so I swing across the four lanes to Beethoven Boulevard off-ramp and just barely am able to make the stop at the bottom, tires screaming and brakes smoking and my foot numb from pounding on the brake pedal. I turn left onto Beethoven and hit the super-charger and get her back up to forty-five with the Porsche still hot behind and then the phone rings and it's Chester.

"Hi Chester, what's up?"

"Nothing boss."

"Well what the hell did you call for?"

"I just called to tell you I'm going to go take a crap."

"Take a what?"

"A crap."

"Well for Christsake go take a crap, you don't have to ask me every time you go take a crap," and I hang up wondering what the hell's got into Chester all of a sudden.

I make a quick right at BEETHOVEN'S FIFTH ALL-NITE LIQUOR MART and wind down Gauguin Court at the legal twenty-five past all the houses and apartments I built last year and then come to the big motel-style apartment which dead-ends the street and which is a three-story pastel pink job with replanted palms and a swimming pool in the central patio. I get more money out of the TAHITI-DELICE PLEASURE APARTMENTS than any other single investment I've got because I've got the thing sewed up nice with that all-night liquor store on the corner which is the stuff that feeds the divorce cases we get out of the TAHITI-DELICE, bugged the way a place can only be

176

bugged when you build it yourself, and boy are some of the cases humdingers.

I slow down real slow and bounce into the TAHITI-DELICE driveway ramp and cruise through like I didn't have a care in the world and as I turn the corner at the parking spaces I notice the Porsche has stopped out on the street and that leaves me free to go on past the parking spaces and hit the driveway of another place I own backing it and in ten seconds I'm out on Hemingway Way and I can just see the Porsche boys running into the TAHITI-DELICE pushing doorbells and wondering where I've gone to.

All this puts me about five minutes late so I hurry past the crackerbox houses to Saint Thomas of Aquinas Avenue and into the bright-light Aquinas commercial strip, a good part of which is my territory. Pretty quick the EMPEROR'S FEAST DRIVE-IN HAMBURGER LOUNGE pops into sight and I slow down and swing right into the parking lot and pull her into the G slot. Before I get out I open up the glove compartment and pull out the jar of Micro-Mice and see that the population has increased by leaps and bounds so I give them a squirt of depopulation virus and also a few grains to eat and shove the works back into the glove compartment.

I climb out of the Kaiser and walk across the parking lot and in the side door of the EMPEROR'S FEAST and am surprised to see Tsvkzov's not there yet. The place's pretty deserted as it usually is at this hour but of

all things seat thirty-eight on the seventy-two-stool
EMPEROR'S FEAST HAMBURGER BAR is occupied by one of
these teen-age girls that looks like an unfinished construction project.

"Okay sweetie," I say, "move it off the stool, it's my
seat."

She turns around and looks at me with a pair of sunglasses so dark it's a wonder she knows which way to look
and takes a piece of unchewed hamburger out of her
mouth with her fingers and drops it right on my left shoe,
the juvenile delinquent.

"Huh?" she says.

"I say you're on my stool."

"Look grampa nobody's sitting in the other fifty stools
that I can see," she says so I guess she can see.

"That may be sweetie but I own this place and I always
sit on stool thirty-eight."

"You own this place?" she says sort of wiggling her
wrist.

"That's what I said."

"Oh. Well maybe you can do something about these
hamburgers. They taste like dead cat."

As a matter of fact we don't use cats in our hamburger
most of the time but I can't give her the news because she
stomps off and out the door which I don't give a damn
about because here you've got to pay before you eat. I
hoist myself up on the stool and run through the menu
which is printed in the formica counter in front of each
stool. As far as I can tell from the remains, the little snot

was eating a PLEASANTBURGER which is the cheapest and weighs a tenth of a pound raw. After that comes the BOURGEOISBURGER at an eighth of a pound and then the DUKEBURGER at a fourth-pound and next the KINGBURGER at a half-pound and the CZARBURGER at a full pound and then the EMPERORBURGER running at two full pounds. Lastly we have at four full pounds the GODBURGER which of course we don't put on the menu. All of these burgers have different size buns and different size onions and to-matoes and lettuce pieces, though the PEASANTBURGER consists of only a half-bun and a meat patty and a tenth of an ounce of mustard in a little plastic cup, and it doesn't come with utensils so the PEASANTBURGER eater always has to ask for utensils and water and most often he asks for a knife to get the mustard out of the little plastic cup as it cannot be otherwise got out without making a big mess. And if he doesn't use the mustard, it just adds to our profit.

After a minute one of the guys behind the counter dressed up as a court dandy comes up and takes my order which is a BOURGEOISBURGER with lots of onions, and he runs off and gets one and brings it right back. I get a glass of water with that and now all I'm missing is Tsvkzov and wonder why he's late. Three teen-age couples come in the door and wobble over to one of the tables and it's pretty clear what they're here for, we've got that too.

I run through my BOURGEOISBURGER pretty damn fast because though it looks big it's the geometric pattern on the plate that does that and it's really pretty damn small, and not too many people order this one because they can't pronounce it which shoves them up to the DUKEBURGER and KINGBURGER class which is where we really begin to make money. So anyway I'm still a bit hungry and whistle for the boy and order a dish of EMPEROR'S ICE CREAM, KINGSIZE, and he brings that.

Just then Tsvkzov whips in the side door and trots across the hamburger pattern carpet and plunks himself down on the stool next to mine.

"Hi Tsvkzov, I've got some hot stuff for you."

"How hot?"

"Damn hot. Sweating hot," I say.

"Too hot?"

"Not if you play it cool."

"All right GASCOYNE, what is this hot stuff?"

"Ha," I say, "I won't let you within ten miles of the stuff until I get an idea of what it's worth. I'd say add ten percent to the red-hot stuff classification and see what sort of rise you get from me."

"That hot, is it?" he asks.

"Damn right."

"All right supposing we offer red-hot stuff plus ten, what do you say?"

"Reimbursement procedures?" I ask.

"Bank draft as usual."

"But how can I be sure?"

"How can we?" he asks.

"Oh you'll be sure all right."

"Well?"

"Ever hear of the Micro-Mouse that's three times smaller and multiplies three times faster than the regular house mouse?"

"Can't say I have," he says.

"You haven't?"

"No," he says. "What the hell are they good for?"

"Eating grain."

"What grain?"

"Your grain, Tsvkzov, Mother Russia's Breadbasket."

"Well now wait a minute," he says. "If these Micro-Mice are three times smaller than regular house mice that means they eat three times less grain, right?"

"Hmm. Well that's one way to look at it but I'm sure not the right way."

"Okay, what other hot stuff have you got GASCOYNE?"

"Well now wait a minute these Micro-Mice—"

"Come on quit pulling my leg," he says.

"I'm not kidding Tsvkzov, these Mice—"

"Ha ha," he says, "why don't you send them to the moon? They say there's a lot of cheese up there."

Well I just about give him one in the dental zone for that but don't because I'm pretty sure he's not the kind to go for the hard sell.

"I may have some news on the Z-bomb next week," I say and it's all pure bull.

"That's more like it. What's the Z-bomb?"

"It's a nuclear-type bomb that destroys only paper, eats the stuff right up in no time, napkins, office paper, money, toilet paper, the works. But I tell you Tsvkzov these Mice

181

are really the last word and that's the honest truth. I can even show you one now.'

"Not worth the bother."

"Look I tell you they're great, fantastic."

"I just can't see it, GASCOYNE."

"Cats can't catch them."

"Why not?" he asks.

"Guess."

"Because they don't want to?"

"No," I say, "guess again."

"Because . . . well, I don't know."

"Oh come on guess."

"GASCOYNE you play too many games with me! Tell me why cats can't catch them, I insist!"

"Calm down Tsvkzov, I'll tell you. Their paws are too big."

"Whose paws?"

"The cats'."

"So. Hmm."

"You see?"

"What exactly do you mean, their paws are too big?"

"Well," I say, "I suppose I mean actually that their claws are too far apart and that the Micro-Mice slip through them."

"Yes I see. And how is this important?"

"Sometimes I think you're dense Tsvkzov, can't you see that if cats can't catch them that pretty soon you'll have Micro-Mice up the ass and eating up the Breadbasket of Mother Russia?"

"Yes that is serious."

"Disastrous."

"But," he says, "I don't understand why you want to sell us some Micro-Mice. I mean we're not going to turn them loose in our own Breadbasket."

"Of course not but with them you will be able to create a Micro-Mouse counterforce rodent deterrent, don't you see?"

"Well there is that point," he says. "What do you want for these animals?"

"Two million for four pair."

"A million and a half."

"Sold," I say.

"How's business?"

"Not so good. How's the wife?"

"Complains about the cold."

"Too bad. Well Tsvkzov how do I get these Mice to you?"

"Oh hell just give them to me."

"Sure," I say wondering why he's getting so sloppy all of a sudden and not liking this attitude but what can I do about it? "They're in the glove compartment of the Kaiser."

"Fine."

He whips out his billfold and takes out a blank bank draft on a Swiss bank and fills in my name and the date and the amount and hands it over to me.

"So long," he says and off he goes without even ordering a hamburger, the cheapskate. I get down off my

stool and go over and sign a presidential voucher without
any guff since I come here pretty often and when I go out
I see the teen-agers smoking happily in the corner. It's
good to have a sort of second home like this for them at
that age.

I hit the parking lot about the time Tsvkzov drives off
in his red Moskvich, a tin can if ever there was one, and I
climb into the Kaiser and have to work up a little sweat
getting the thing started because the battery's gone low
for some reason though it seems to charge all right as soon
as I get the engine running. Could be she got a little too
hot on the last run and started to tighten up as soon as I
stopped.

I back her up and then throw her in drive and bounce
onto the avenue right and fiddle with the rearview to
check the scenery out back and damn if there isn't a little
red Porsche right smack on my tail and I slow down to
catch the license number and about lose my uppers when
I see that it's got the same number as the blue Porsche
and the silver one before that. All I can think is that
somebody who can have three cars under the same license
number has got a hell of a lot of pull somewhere, and it
sure isn't one of O'Mallollolly's crew because I know just
how much pull he has and exactly where he has it and it
doesn't go so far as three sets of identical license plates by
a long shot. About this point I get real interested and
wonder where in the hell these visiting firemen are
coming from, nowhere I know about.

∗

I give Chester a ring.

"Chester what's the—"

"*Aaah-choua!*" he interrupts. "Excuse me boss, got a cold."

"Well the best thing's to take an aspirin and just go on like nothing's the matter with you."

"Sure boss," he says.

"Now Chester I want you to cable Tsvkzov's bank as usual and see that he's got the funds to cover his latest check for a million and a half. Next, what did you ever find out about that Porsche's license number I gave you?"

"Not a damn thing more boss. Reggie in State Automobile Registration says there's no record of it up there except what he sent us and that's just three items, the make, the year and license number. No motor number or anything."

"Wow. Somebody's messing around up there. I'll have to take care of that next week. What else's new?"

"Nothing good," he says. "The fifth floor of Police Tower has surrendered and from what little I can find out O'Mallollolly's running the whole place now."

"I was afraid of that. Well we'll get by."

"And the feds caught Flash Fingers."

"What?"

"Seems that instead of putting all the cash he got out of the WESTBINDER vault back into the mail for us he kept some for himself and the feds traced it in about five hours."

"But hell all the bank records burned up," I say.

185

"No, the Federal Reserve had a record of all currency sent to the WESTBINDER that day."

"Damn, well I guess all we can do is get him a lawyer. Now Chester before I forget it again I want you to check up completely on the Apotheosis Life Insurance Company and I want to know everything about why they issued Policy Number 9354728 to Rufus Roughah in spite of the heavy risk. Seems to me I've heard of this company somewhere but I can't remember where. But wait a minute, before you get into that, give Nuddard a call and tell him to have the whole front page cleared off and ready for when I give him the material which I've still got to think about some. Don't suppose there's any chance left of getting Roughah's body out of Cold Storage."

"No boss, to tell you the truth with the shuffling around that's going on at Police Tower I don't have any idea what numbers to dial anymore."

"Well we'll just have to do without Roughah then."

Which isn't so bad as it sounds since we've got Grant the butler's body and it's just a matter of a little framework for the benefit of the insurance company and the newspaper reading public, though without Police Tower it's going to be a bit of a trick to pull off. I've got to get O'Mallollolly out soon, that's all there is to it because if he wants to throw a monkey wrench into my works he might just be able to pull it off and I begin to wonder how I got myself into this sort of fix which I haven't been in since more time than I can remember, for being so goddamn soft no doubt. But I'm not going to show my hand until

I'm dead sure what O'Mallollolly is up to and one thing's sure and that is that I want to know why he wants to run the whole damn town when he knows he hasn't got the brains or backing for this size operation. Something's screwed up somewhere.

I zip under the Turnpike Tollroad underpass but of course I'm not going to take the tollroad because I absolutely refuse to pay another cent to officials I'm subsidizing strongly in other ways, so I keep on Clyde Hopkins Bird Sanctuary Road which angles back toward the center of town. I'm wondering all the time in the back of my mind who to put in O'Mallollolly's place when I pry him out and the trouble is MacGanymede's dead and there's nobody else I really trust in the Tower and somebody from outside would be all right up until they got corrupted, which happens pretty fast. No trouble getting them in, all I do is give the Mayor the name to appoint which will make him happy because it'll show the electorate his paralytic stroke hasn't affected his mind yet. Poor bastard all he can do is wiggle his ears and the only thing that keeps him alive is the thought of being reelected maybe for the pleasure of being carried in and out of his office every day. I could always have him appoint himself Police Commissioner but the trouble is I don't have the time to pull all the strings in this damn town, I've got too much going on right now to keep track of.

Suddenly Roughah's red Rolls goes flashing by me in the slow lane with Dmitri the chauffeur at the wheel and nobody I can see in the back, and I get the feeling he

187

didn't see me. Then before I can chew this one over Nancy flashes by in her blue Lancia and I don't think she saw me either so they must be in a big hurry about something and I'm interested to see what, besides wanting to ask them both a few questions. I snap on the supercharger and run her up to sixty to catch up, quite a bit over the limit but the afternoon traffic rush hasn't started yet. In a minute we come to the Bird Sanctuary-Mirindaranda wye and all hit the signal green and slip onto Mirindaranda Road heading straight for the Roughah digs so it's pretty clear where they're going. I slow down a little and give Chester a ring because I've got the scoop for Nuddard all sorted out in my mind now.

"Chester is that you?"

"No this is Frank."

"Damn where's Chester?"

"He wasn't feeling well and said something about going out for some more pills for his shooting pains."

"Holy shit! Tell him to call me the moment he gets back."

"Who's this?"

"GASCOYNE, you asshole."

"Yes sir! Excuse me!"

Miserable incompetents, what a time for shooting pains. How can you get shooting pains sitting at a desk and telephone all day?

We hit the Mirindaranda split and Dmitri goes on and slides the Rolls into the garage and while I cruise by slowly, Nancy double-parks in front of it and jumps out screaming and waving her fists and they both go up the outside stairs. I drop the Kaiser into an alley and turn off the phone and then hotfoot it over to the garage and peek inside and see a stairway in there which I remember leads up to Dmitri's kitchen upstairs, just what I need. I tiptoe up and of all the lucky things the door's unlocked and so I inch it open real quiet and creep inside. From the noise it sounds like they're in the bedroom having a tiff and I work my way down the hall and put my ear against the door but can't make anything out but of course that's not the way to do it. I take my old Zenith hearing aid out of my shirt pocket and turn it up high and press it against the door and that really picks up the vowels and consonants.

". . . only when you give me my house back," Nancy's saying, almost screaming.

"It's in little pieces, you idiot, and you'll never get it back," he says.

"Well build me a new one."

"We're broke, flat broke, understand? Can't you see that if you just tell us what you know we may be able to find it and then we can build you a whole housing tract of houses."

"If only I could trust you Dmitri," she says.

"You don't need to trust me. You don't even need to tell me. Tell some other member of the corporation."

"What corporation?"

"I'm part of a corporation registered in the state and created for the sole purpose of finding Roughah's treasure trove. We were capitalized at three hundred thousand but we've used that all up. We're flat broke. You've got to help us Nancy or we'll be ruined."

"Maybe that's what I want," she says.

"You little bitch!"

There's a slap and a crash and a little scream and I think it's best to make my presence known so I put my hearing aid back and turn it down to normal and whip out my automatic and unscrew the safety and fling open the door and dash through. I find Dmitri about to give Nancy another slap and he has his gun out and is unfortunately facing square at me. He sees me and says, "All right drop your gun GASCOYNE."

Which is really my line he's stealing but then I suddenly remember that I emptied my gun into the Widow Roughah's living room wall and sure as hell forgot to reload it so I don't really need it. But what possesses me to drop it on my toe with the corn on it is beyond me, and I've dropped quite a few guns in my life but never has this happened before. I double up with pain and Dmitri puts a hole in the wall where I was. I never did like the guy.

"All right GASCOYNE, on your feet and don't try anything else funny because I've got a short temper at the moment."

"So I noticed."

I stand up and lean against the wall to ease the burning pain in my foot, thinking that this sort of thing wouldn't happen if I had a string running from the butt of my automatic to my belt like a watch fob, ought to patent that one.

"It's very convenient you're here now GASCOYNE, since you're the man I wanted to talk to and so suppose you start talking fast."

"About what?"

"Roughah's treasure trove."

"First time I've heard of it," I say.

"Cut the comedy."

"Look I'm not kidding."

"We'll see," he says.

He goes to a closet and pulls out a big black bullwhip. Nancy gives a little screaming gasp and frankly I'm about ready to pee in my pants. If there's one thing I can't stand it's people using force against me. Really pisses me off.

"Now wait a minute," I say, "you just be careful with that thing, you never know quite how it's going to land."

"I know exactly," he says, uncoiling it.

"That's what I was afraid of. Don't I get one too?"

"No, sorry, there aren't enough to go around."

He starts warming the thing up with snakelike movements.

"Okay Dmitri you know damn well Roughah had no treasure trove. His estate's almost bankrupt as it is."

"Yeah, that's something else I wanted to know. Why?"

"Beats me."

"Sure it does."

Well he gives this bullwhip a nasty swing and picks up a heavy cast-iron ashtray with it about two inches away from my hand and flicks it through a window opening out on the street. There's a thud below and a groan and then the sound of somebody falling down.

"Okay," he says, "an ear or a nose?"

"Well now let's not get excited," I say. "What was your question?"

"Where did all Roughah's money go?"

"He didn't have a hell of a lot to begin with, about half a million more or less liquid," I say, "and this was managed by FLEESON AND BAIGHT, a combined investment and accounting firm."

"And?"

"Well I suspect they managed it badly, Roughah didn't have a head for anything besides rackets, or else they siphoned it off for their own use and fabricated monthly statements to keep Roughah happy which wasn't hard because he's one of those people who expect to lose money if a deal looks at all honest."

"Come on GASCOYNE, that sounds nice but a little fuzzy. This FLEESON AND BAIGHT firm, who are they?"

"What do you mean, who are they?"

"Who's back of them?" he asks.

"Why should anybody be back of them?"

"Ah cut it out GASCOYNE." He gives the whip a nasty wiggle.

"All right Dmitri, I'm FLEESON AND BAIGHT."

"Okay that makes sense at last. So it's you that's been siphoning off Roughah's fortune for the last fifteen years, that does make sense. How much you make GASCOYNE?"

192

"About six million I reckon," I say.

"You get it all?"

"No," I say, "I think we only got about a third. I think he stashed the rest away. Gold or diamonds, I'd say," I say.

"Or a Swiss bank account."

The trouble is I've got the lousy gold coin right there in my pocket.

"No," I say, "I think he distrusted banks, even Swiss ones."

Dmitri fondles the bullwhip.

"About twelve million, you think GASCOYNE?"

"I'd say."

"That's what I figured too about the time I decided the real wheel was Roughah and not you GASCOYNE and that there was real money backing him. You're made out of paper GASCOYNE. You look big but you're really not, and so when I thought about this I saw that the truth was that you were a convenient front for Roughah to hide behind. And then knowing Roughah I knew he would do something stupid with his money, like bury it where any idiot could get at it. All right GASCOYNE—"

But then he's interrupted by some character down on the street below bellowing like hell and saying, "Hey up there next time you throw ashtrays out the window give us a little warning, huh?"

"Oh go shove it!" Dmitri yells. "Okay now GASCOYNE I know you've got the bank account number, now let's have it."

He raises his bullwhip for what appears to be an honest-to-God offensive against my left ear and then all of a sudden that cast-iron ashtray comes flying back in the window and catches Dmitri right in the side of the head and he crumples to the floor. "John Doe," he gasps and gives up the ghost. He deserved it. Made the same mistake a lot of people make in this town, thinking I'm not the wheel. What they imagine is someone just like me right behind me, but there's nobody there but us chickens, ha ha.

Well that's that and it leaves me alone with Nancy who I've been wanting to talk to for a good while.

"Okay Nancy—" I start to say but she gives me a slap across the eater that's far from pleasant. "What's that for?" I ask.

"For stealing Rufus's money, crummy bastard."

"That's ancient history. Come on Nancy you know a couple of things I'd like to know so let's hear them."

"Just like that?"

"Why not?" I ask.

"You mean you're not even going to offer me anything?"

"Hell no. I never pay money for information in advance. If I get it and it's any good I pay after."

"How much?" she asks.

"I decide that too. Anywhere from ninety-nine cents to nine hundred and ninety-nine dollars."

"It doesn't really matter anyway. I'm not going to tell you a thing," she says.

194

"Why not?"

"Because I just can't stand your guts, GASCOYNE."

Then she turns on her heels and marches out of the place in a way I find pretty irritating because I want to know what she knows and she's going to find it damn tough in the future if she doesn't start cooperating now. I pick up my automatic and run down the stairs after her but she's already in the car leaving rubber hotly on the pavement and the Kaiser's way in the alley across the street. Still I think it worth a try so I run across the street on the double and jump in the Kaiser and start her up but the gear linkage gets stuck as it often does and I can't throw her in reverse to back up, which means Nancy gets away this time.

As soon as I catch my breath, and I ought to keep that running down if not cut it out altogether, I give Chester a ring.

"Chester?"

"Yeah boss."

"What the hell do you mean by leaving the phone again like that at a time like this?"

"I had to get some more pills boss. These shooting pains are awful."

"It's all in your goddamn head and if you leave that phone once more you're finished, understand?"

"But boss I tried to call but the line was busy."

"Hell it was busy!"

"Well I don't know then, I must have dialed the wrong

Gascoyne

number. But boss I tell you, honestly, I've got to take a rest pretty soon. I'm about to drop."

"All right you can take a rest. How about Saturday?" I ask.

"Jesus boss that's two days away. I don't know even whether I can make it through tonight."

"Sure you can Chester."

"No boss, I've just got to take a rest. I'll try to hang on till six this evening but not any longer."

"Now Chester nobody gives me an ultimatum in this town, you know damn well."

He doesn't say anything for a second.

"Hell boss I don't give a plugged nickel whether anybody does or not, I'm stopping at six this evening and that's that. I've been up fifty-three hours straight and I've had it and I'm not taking any more of it."

"Well now think about it Chester, I wouldn't do anything rash. Just think about it a little bit and you'll change your mind, I'm sure."

He stays quiet again.

"Okay Chester what's new?"

More silence there is.

"Come on cut the crap, what's new?" I say getting a little more than peeved.

"A couple of little bitty items, that's all," he says and coughs. "The first one is Mark called and says you're out of the housing tract and freeway deal because he can't take a chance on something like that. Also nobody wants the three hundred jeeps so you've just bought yourself

196

three hundred jeeps. O'Mallollolly keeps calling and wanting to know why you're still in town and promises to run you out if you wait much longer. And then there's always Louis."

"What about Louis?"

"They nabbed him with two and a half million in heroin and word has it he might start telling stories. Spread the rap-around, as they say, to get a little time off for himself."

"You're kidding aren't you Chester?"

"Nope I'm telling the honest truth."

"Hmm. Things aren't looking up are they?"

"No boss can't say they are."

"Well we've got work to do anyway. First off I want you to send the Body Snatching Flying Squad from the GREEN FERN AND LILY BLOSSOM PARLOR OF FINAL REPOSE over to pick up Dmitri's body, he got it in the head, and have them do it up fancy and send the bills to the Widow Roughah and any next of kin.

"Now I want you to take this down and relay it direct to Nuddard for the editorial page of the special late-afternoon *Red Flash Herald.* Here goes: 'Good journalism and justice have kept our mouths shut about the bad stink coming out of one of our city's famous landmarks which is Police Tower. But now the cat has gotten out of the bag and it turns out to be a full-blown polecat and we can't keep our mouths shut any longer. Now the enlightened public crying for facts and the truth is going to get it and we are hoping that a little public discussion will clear the air, but it's going to take more than that. The trouble is, is it going to do any good to just talk when it turns out that Police Commissioner O'Mallollolly who's supposed to watch our children is caught red-handed embezzling ninety-nine percent of the Policeman's Pension Fund and when it can be proven that certain nasty things are going on in the lavatories of Police Tower which is fast becoming a pillar of perversion? No and that isn't all. Most of you are probably wondering about the death under mysterious circumstances of Rufus Roughah, prominent citizen among other things, and wondering still more about our Police Commissioner's verdict of suicide. Well wonder no more because this newspaper has obtained the complete truth which is that Rufus Roughah was murdered by none other than Police Commissioner O'Mallollolly or one of his paid henchmen, for reasons everybody can guess, namely that Roughah was on the verge of uncovering the scandalous state of affairs in Police Tower and was preparing to expose O'Mallollolly to the unmerciful eye of the public. Roughah died in the pursuit of justice, a real martyr, and we are proud to carry on his work, so as we see it it is a time for public action and now the public must join hands and throw out the tyrants and put down their tyranny. As somebody said, and Nuddard please find out who said it, Taxation without Representation is Tyranny, and what do you call it when you are paying the taxes of the very people who are your tyrants? We call it Communism and if that word strikes terror in your hearts you know what you must do. Stand up and be counted Mr. John Q. Public because now is the time to show the stuff you are made of. Go to it and God be with you! Get all that on tape Chester?"

"Sure boss. Recorder's on all the time."

"All right, tell Nuddard to clean that up whatever way he wants it for the editorial, just so long as he keeps the basic ideas. Now I want the complete words of the 'Star-Spangled Banner' put in a little box under the editorial and tell Nuddard to use all of the first and second pages for the scandal story. From what I've just given him he can make up all the details he wants. He's free to use his imagination and have him call me direct if he has any questions. You can give him my number Chester."

"No kidding."

"A little something extra for him. I want the Scandal of '65 to be a real humdinger."

I hang up and drop the thing into Drive and roll down the alley and come out on Mirindaranda Road South just before the split and cross and get back into Mirindaranda Road heading east. I'm thinking that when Nuddard gets the *Red Flash Herald* out which will be damn soon O'Mallollolly will suddenly find life not so easy anymore and will begin to wonder how he got himself into such a fix, but he can't say he didn't know it was coming. The Scandal of '59 was so good they almost gave Nuddard some journalism prize and I hope he makes it this time. Old MacWigo, the poor bastard, never knew what hit him, but O'Mallollolly's seen this one coming from a way off and I'd sure pay a lot to see him when it hits him square in the face.

The *Red Flash Herald* ought to hit the streets about six or seven this evening which will make the regular evening edition a little late but they'll sure get their money's worth. I think a follow-up in the morning *Sunshine Special Times* and then the regular morning *Times* will keep the fire hot and the fireworks themselves ought to start about noon tomorrow with riots and picketing and other demonstrations, working in somewhere the old unbeatable angle, police brutality, compromising photos all over the place. Just then Marge calls.

"Hi Marge. Well how's Condor's Crag?"

"I haven't got there yet."

"What? Jesus Christ Marge let's get off the dime. At the rate you're going the place'll be in ruins by the time you get there."

"Well please dear I can't help it if that stupid car you gave me broke down again. I'm not a master mechanic you know, if you want—"

"Now calm down Marge you know damn well that car's breaking down because you're not driving it properly like they told you at the garage."

"Told me at the garage? Don't make me laugh dear. They didn't tell me a damn thing. They just put the keys into my clammy fist and knocked me down on the ground and then stuffed me in the driver's seat and the next thing

I know I'm at Crankcase Summit with a blown something."

"Calm down Marge. Where are you now?"

"I'm at a little gas station on the north end of Lake Lobotomples with a frozen generator bearing. The little man at the garage tells me they haven't even started to make the part yet in England."

"Now calm down Marge, how does he know?"

"Quit telling me to calm down dammit!"

"Well you should be able to get the car all the way home without the generator if you don't use the lights."

"That's what Tom says," she says.

"Who's Tom? You're not alone?"

"You think I'd travel alone in this country with a car like this?"

"Well who's this Tom?"

"He's the bartender at the FAT PHEASANT AND OLD GREYHOUNDE, a very nice boy who's off the rest of today and so I invited him along for the ride."

"Really Marge you shouldn't pick up strange men like that," I say even though he's an employee of mine. You never know about people who work for you.

"He's not a strange man, he's not even a man. He's only twenty-two, a mere child."

"Well I don't know about that Marge."

"Well I don't give a damn about what you don't know about or what you know about but I do know you sent me on this picnic and you knew damn well there was going to be ants in the honey and you're just out of your mind to think you can sit down there and direct the traffic by long-distance phone," she says.

"What did you mean by that?"

"Just what I said, that's what I mean."

"Whatever you meant, I wouldn't say things like that if I were you," I say.

"You're not."

"Now wait a minute Marge there's a note of hostility there and I want to know what you mean by it."

"Not a thing," she says.

"What do you mean, not a thing? What are you trying to say?" I ask.

"Nothing. Not a thing."

"Now Marge stop that and let's talk this over like two reasonable human beings."

"No. I don't want to talk."

"Why not?" I ask.

"I just don't want to talk, that's all. Goodbye," she says.

"Wait a minute."

"Goodbye."

"Just a minute!" I say. "Are you still there?"

"Goodbye."

"Now look when you calm down again all I want you to do is to go up to Condor's Crag—"

"I can't. Goodbye."

"Wait! Why not?" I ask.

"I can't. Goodbye."

"Hey Marge!"

Then it's quiet but she hasn't hung up and then there's a clanking around the phone and that seashell sound when somebody puts their hand over the receiver and finally a man's voice.

"Hallo Mr. GASCOYNE, this here's Tom Rasper."

"Yes Mr. Rasper?"

"Well Mr. GASCOYNE Miss Margie wants me to tell you there that she cain't go up to that Condor's Craig place on account of there's been a lanslaad all over the road from barrow pit to barrow pit."

"I see. Well now wait a minute Mr. Rasper you just tell her she can walk. Where is this landslide?"

"Right at the bottom there where you turn off the main road to go up to the Condor place."

"Of course she can walk. It's only two miles. You tell her that."

"Well I'll try and ask her Mr. GASCOYNE. Hold on there a sec and I'll be right back."

He slaps his hand over the receiver for one hell of a long time and then he comes back.

"Mr. GASCOYNE well Miss Margie says she'll do that haike all right if she can stay another naight in the Wolverine on the way back."

"On the way back? I see. Well Mr. Rasper I don't know about that."

"Well Mr. GASCOYNE I know it's not my place and none of my business at all to pass out advaice to total strangers,

203

so I do beg your pardon when I say Miss Margie here won't have it any other way. I give you my word of honor on that."

"Well all right then, but she can stay only if she takes the cheap room downstairs."

"Oh now Mr. GASCOYNE I wouldn't put my mother-in-law's maiden aunt in that room, honestly. It ain't fit for a dawg."

"Well it couldn't be as bad as all that," I say.

"All right Mr. GASCOYNE I'll ask Miss Margie here if she wants to stay in that filthy dark little room."

"Thanks."

Then there's a short silence.

"Mr. GASCOYNE I'm afraid Miss Margie here has got the aidea that she'd laike to stay in the bridal suite tonight."

"Bridal suite? Now Mr. Rasper you just tell her—"

"Please accept my pardon for interrupting you laike this sir, but since I reluctantly faind myself in the middle between the two of you, I can see that nobody at all is going to be happy here unless you give poor little Miss Margie here what she has her heart set on. I mean man to man, Mr. GASCOYNE, Miss Margie's an awfully naice woman but she's got this streak in her and unless you give her what she wants she'll never stop asking for what she cain't have."

"All right Mr. Rasper. She can have the bridal suite."

"Thank you ever so kaindly Mr. GASCOYNE, I, oh just a sec now."

A little silence there is.

"Miss Margie here also wants to thank you Mr. GASCOYNE."

"I see. Well thank you for your help Mr. Rasper."

"Pleasure's mine to be sure."

Well I don't know about this Tom Rasper type but there are times when you have to take advantage of people you wouldn't otherwise talk to even and Marge does throw these fits over nothing at all now and then. About now I find myself driving down Mirindaranda Road a good clip and suddenly wonder where I'm going in such a goddamn hurry and so I slow down and take it easy for awhile. Then it dawns on me that I don't really have anywhere to go right now which doesn't happen very often, last time about five years ago, and I wonder what's brought on this kettle of fish. Me GASCOYNE with nothing to do, they ought to put that in the headlines. Usually in the wee hours of the morning things get pretty slow and I can't do much but that's because everybody insists on wasting a third of their day sleeping, so what I often do between three and five A.M. is pop into one of my all-night drive-in movie places and watch the flicks but right now the sun's still up. Nothing else to do so I catch the green arrow left and run up Crumble Canyon Drive for kicks which is a pretty posh part of town to live in now and I could see that one coming twenty years ago so I was smart enough to snatch up a lot of the high ground when there wasn't anything but rabbits and gophers and rattlesnakes using it, but I myself prefer to live in a house trailer over near the airport. I always like to have a couple of wheels under me though I hardly use the joint except for a nap now and then and to fry an egg.

Crumble Canyon Drive starts getting pretty steep so I drop her in low and run past all the fancy houses, sitting ducks for landslides and mudslides and brush fires but that's the kind of thing these people really eat up, and then I notice the Kaiser's getting hot in a nasty way so I slow her down to about fifteen and give the rearview a jiggle. Right behind me I see I've got a string of Cadillacs and Continentals and Imperials all waiting for a straight stretch to pass me on but I don't give a damn because half of them are probably leased from me anyway and the other half financed by the CRUMBLE CANYON SAVINGS AND LOAN, but what does get me is that little red Porsche behind all them which I've forgotten all about, getting careless in my old age. Well there isn't much I can do about it and I'll just let this one stay on because I've got the unpleasant feeling that if I shake him off another one'll pop out from behind the next bush which is a state of affairs I can't do much about until I find out who the joker is behind it all, like it or not.

Near the top of the ridge we're climbing the engine starts missing like mad and it sounds like the timing's going wild and if that's more than steam leaking through the hood joints I'm in bad trouble. Still I've got to keep going and I make the first level stretch at the top and drop her back into drive and speed her up a little to cool the engine while the Crumble Canyon touring club roars past me with their painted women looking out the side windows at me like they're afraid I'm going to be their new neighbor or something. I get the Kaiser up to thirty now and putt along Bigview Ridge Road and the temp drops some but not enough though the steam stops and I can relax a little to take a gander at the view which is not bad today for a change since the air's clear and the sun's getting ready to set.

The houses finally run out and then I roll past a bunch of land I haven't cleared the brush off yet and come to Bigview Park and decide to pull into the Bigview Park Panoramic View Spot Parking Lot which gives a lovely view of the whole shooting match and what's more important there's a faucet and a hose there. I lease these thirty acres to the city, which put up the park and keeps it maintained because they think I'm going to give it to them in ten years or something but they're all wrong because I'm waiting for people to move in next to the park and then when the area is a nice jammed-up suburb all around Bigview Park I'll clear out all the damn bushes and throw up one of my BONANZA-BANQUETTE shopping centers which'll probably start making money even before it opens.

I pull the Kaiser in which has started up boiling again and stop her and get out with the motor running and open up the hood. Then I go get the hose and turn it on and give the radiator a good hosing down which causes a big white cloud of steam but stops the boiling pretty fast. I unscrew the radiator cap and discover the thing's only half full and wonder why but a quick look at the hose running from the engine head to the radiator is enough to solve that one, the damn thing's got a nasty split in it, just bought the thing too, a BIG DADDY SPECIAL it was.

I hoof it around to the trunk and unlock it and pull out my tool box and throw off the lid and pull out a roll of friction tape which I take back to the radiator and wind around the split hose. Won't last forever but I keep a full jeep can of water in the back and if I take it easy it shouldn't leak too much. I take the tape back and while I'm messing around in the trunk I open up a can of BIG DADDY SUPER SWELL KOLA with that magic ingredient that makes the kids really lap it up can after can and tank myself up and throw the can under an oleander bush for the squirrels to eat. Finally I close the whole works up and get back in the car and feel a little drowsy, so time to retire as they say and I push back the seat and slouch down and hit the hay.

I wake up ten minutes later but frankly don't feel any better at all, maybe even a little tireder. I pull the seat up and just about start up the engine when the view sort of catches my eye and so hell why not just sit a minute, I don't have anywhere to go. A few lights are beginning to come on down there in the city and the shadows are getting deep so that the freeways and expressways and skyways show up real nice around the masses of houses and buildings all sort of glued together in the distance except for Police Tower with its fifteen stories lit up like a Christmas tree and GASCOYNE CENTER at the other end of town

208

but not lit up yet because the only window in the place is the one out of my office. They look the same height from here and it doesn't show that GASCOYNE CENTER is seven feet shorter except that if you count the radio-TV tower GASCOYNE CENTER is taller though most people don't count that. The trouble is everybody remembers GASCOYNE CENTER is seven feet shorter. One-track mind the public has. I'd slap a couple of extra stories onto the top except that the idiot architect didn't provide for it structurally. Last thing he ever built in this town. Just then Chester calls.

"What's up Chester?"

"I got the information on the Apotheosis Insurance Company and the Roughah policy. Sure you want to hear it boss?" he says in the sort of tone of voice that makes me worry.

"Go ahead shoot," I say.

"Well it seems—" he says but gets interrupted by a wheeze and a gasp and a little choking sound.

"You all right Chester?" I ask, it sounds like an act to me.

"Sure boss, just one of my shooting pains. Well anyway this company was set up especially to insure Roughah, not legal of course, which means the idea was to squeeze fat premiums out of Roughah without intending to pay up if Roughah kicked the bucket. The gimmick was that Apotheosis said it would be the middle man and reinsure Roughah with a lot of other companies with small policies but it never did this, just kept the premiums."

"Yes."

"Well fine and dandy, but the character," he says gasping and coughing again, "but the fellow who set the company up put some bright-eyed college graduate to run the thing and this kid gets the idea to go straight and make the whole operation legal, especially because the wheel behind it all keeps out of the way as long as Roughah's payments are pushed on to him."

"Yes."

"Well the kid changes the name of the company and starts making a little honest money when all of a sudden Roughah goes and gets himself killed."

"Yes."

"And this means that if it's proven that Roughah was murdered and didn't commit suicide the Apotheosis Life Insurance Company owes Nadine Roughah a cool million which it doesn't have and that means the whole swindle comes out in the bankruptcy proceedings."

"I get the picture Chester. What was the original name of—"

"THE RESURRECTION ASSURANCE COMPANY which is in our files boss and we're checking it up now."

"That's enough Chester."

Damn my lousy memory. It was me back in '53 that set up RESURRECTION ASSURANCE and that means if I prove Roughah was murdered I'm the one who gets screwed, goddamn. This one really throws me down and walks all over me. Especially since it's partly my fault. So many damn things going on these last ten years I can't keep them straight anymore. Getting too old. But damn it wasn't my fault that Johnny-A got himself killed in '57 and I had to replace him with Chester the half-wit. And then that asshole college kid who has to go change the name of the company and for the worse of course. He ought to know that people who buy life insurance in this world can't pronounce Apotheosis. Let people alone one minute and they go get a bright idea and ruin everything.

Well so much for the Roughah case, I guess I'll just have to write that one off. Bad days happen. Nothing to do but keep on going and wait for the next good one. Somehow tomorrow looks good. O'Mallollolly will be out by then and I'll go back and see the Widow Roughah and we'll have a little talk about the little gold coin. I begin to think Dmitri's last words—John Doe—could be the name under which the Swiss bank account is held, even though that it's a bank account number isn't proven yet, and I'll see if she's interested in buying a little information. But still it's hard to get over having wasted two whole days on the Roughah thing.

Well there's only one thing to do when things get like this and that's go home and take a snooze and have a bite to eat, not that I really need it but it might cheer me up some. I haven't seen my old fourteen-foot HOLLY ROLLER MOBILE HOME, custom made, for about three weeks now and a cold shower might just do the trick even if I can't sleep. I usually just lie on the couch and listen to the jets coming in and taking off, nice racket they make.

Gascoyne

I push the starter button and the thing catches but it takes a hell of a long time to get the engine started which happens when it overheats like that, floods I think. I race it a little to clear out all the crud and she throws a nice cloud of exhaust all over the landscape and I plunk her into reverse but damn if the linkage doesn't jam again and there I am right up against the curb and my physique is such I couldn't move this heap pushing or pulling with a block and tackle in ten years and there's not a damn soul in sight. Not my day.

Well the hell with it and I throw it in low and floor it and the front end leaps over the curb and then the back bounces over and there's this awful crunching and crashing and then *bla-bla-bla-bla* which just keeps on going so I know what I've just lost is the muffler. All this time too I'm crashing through the oleander bushes and hedges and lawns of Bigview Park as fast as I can so I don't get stuck in the mud because they've just watered it, and I'm trying to find a path or service road out. I keep going through and mowing down the shrubbery and then I break out into a big circular lawn and drive around that leaving tracks about five inches deep but can't find any way out so I pick a part of the bushes doesn't look so bad and floor it and crash into it, mud and pieces of lawn flying everywhere and then bushes and branches scraping and scratching and snapping and the motor going *bla-bla-bla-bla*. Then I hit another little clearing and flush out a couple of teen-agers, whatever the hell they're doing there, and finally fall into a ditch that seems three feet deep at

212

least but fortunately I'm going fast enough that I bounce right out of it onto a dirt road, stopping just in time to keep from falling into the ditch on the other side, but I banged my knee pretty bad on the steering column.

At least the engine's still running so I climb out and limp around the car to see what the damage is. A lot of paint's gone but there wasn't much left anyway and the left headlight got poked out and I lost a good part of the left rear fender which was pretty rusted out anyway, damn dogs always peeing back there. But the tires are okay, that's what counts, so I hop back in and put her in drive and head for Bigview Ridge Road and when I hit that I have to wait a hell of a long time to turn left because the rush hour's on full blast now.

I get her going finally and right off pick up the red Porsche which was hiding behind a pepper tree or something, well I just don't give a damn. Then I think I hear the phone ringing but am not sure so I turn back up my hearing aid and it is. I pick up the receiver and it's Chester but I can't understand a damn thing with all the racket so I pull over to the side of the road and shut off the engine.

"Boss are you there?"

"Yeah Chester. The muffler went out. That's what—"

"Nuddard won't print the editorial or anything."

"Won't *what?*"

"He won't do it boss."

"He's fired!"

"I think he's already resigned."

"Goddamn he can't do this to me. I own that newspaper and I own every newspaper in town and he can't just walk out on me like that, who does he think he is? Chester find somebody to put out that newspaper and quick!"

"I can't boss."

"You can't?"

"I've tried boss. Stevens on the TV stations won't touch it and has resigned and so has what's-his-name on the radio stations. There's nobody boss."

"You do it Chester!"

"Boss the whole damn newspaper staff has walked out."

"Shit!"

"And that's not all—"

"What?" I ask.

"O'Mallollolly's got the CENTER surrounded with God knows how many cops. This has been going on for a half hour but nobody up here knew about it until just—"

"He can't do that either! Call the Mayor and have him fire O'Mallollolly, my orders."

"The Mayor's been kidnapped."

This is awful. Just awful. I calm myself down and nibble on a Ritz cracker.

"Okay Chester you've got to act fast and clean now if we're going to get out of this one at all. I want you to go down to the fourteenth floor, no don't leave the phone, send Wesley down with *signed orders* to start burning Records and Documents, everything there. Some of the people have been there long enough so they remember when we got scared in '51 and burned all the papers. The

214

incinerator will hold about three filing cabinets at a time, start with File X and tell them to go slow and do a good job, not to hurry. All right?"

"Yeah. One more thing."

"Yes?"

"Tsvkzov's closed out his bank account. That check he gave you is worthless."

"The prick!"

I hang up and just sit there by the side of the road with cars rushing by every which way and me wondering how the hell this is happening to me and how I can stop it from keeping on happening. I get the awful feeling that something's been going on behind my back for a longer time than I care to think about and all this is happening according to somebody's plan, and I'd say O'Mallollolly's the one and that he's bought up the town but I happen to know that he hasn't even paid for his own house and in fact he even missed last month's payment. Somebody really big must be back of him but nobody in town I know of is that big and nobody in the whole damn state either. It doesn't make sense and it makes me sick. Here I had things running smoothly and everybody happy and now everything goes haywire for no good reason at all. Makes you lose your faith in human nature.

I start the Kaiser back up and throw her into drive and push my way into the traffic mess and decide now's the time for long shots and one good idea comes to me right away, and that's having the morning *Times* printed upstate by the *Capital Tribune* end of the chain and having the whole edition shipped down by special plane. It'll be late but better than never.

I pull back over to the side of the road and turn off the motor and give Chester a ring.

"Yeah?" somebody says.

"Who's this?"

"William."

"William who?" I ask.

"Bowman."

"Oh. Where the hell's Chester?"

"You mean that guy that was here at the phone a minute ago?"

"Yes."

"Funny thing happened."

"*What?*"

"A minute ago he just keeled over. Dead as a doornail."

"Oh no!"

"Yep! Heart attack or something. They're laying him out in the next office."

Hot damn, that really does fix my wagon right down to the last nut and bolt! I knew that ass had an unreliable streak in him and now what am I supposed to do? I don't know a damn phone number in this town except his and Marge's and the Roughahs', couldn't even call the Fire Department. Well GASCOYNE I say to myself, you've got yourself in a real fix this time, but there's no sense crying over spilt milk, so I start up the engine and pull onto the road, hell with them all, and make an illegal U-turn right in the teeth of some Cadillac and head right toward town to take matters into my own hands. I may be cutting my own throat this way but that's a chance I've got to take while I've still got a chance to take chances. At the rate I'm going it won't be long.

I turn right at Flashflood Gulch Lane and head down the long twisting hill toward town as fast as the old Kaiser can take it, tires howling and bouncing on the curves and the thing backfiring like mad because I think something went out of tune when it heated up. Well the old buggy's got a lot of miles on her and I'm so generally pissed off I'd do something really extravagant and call what's-his-name —can't even remember that now—at the agency and have him get out a new Imperial and ready for me except that little matter of not having his phone number handy, and I don't think he knows my voice anyway. Scares me a little. Never seen me either.

I blast some guy on a motorscooter out of the way with my air horn and hit the bottom of Flashflood Gulch Lane and turn left onto Ben Hur Boulevard heading straight downtown to GASCOYNE CENTER which has the outside floodlights on now but some asshole forgot to turn on the GASCOYNE CENTER neon light on top just below the radio-TV tower. He'll be fired soon enough with a lot of other farts. The only trouble with this free enterprise system is that you have to pay a lot of people and this costs a hell of a lot of money to the employer as I ought to know and what do you get out of it but a lot of nonsense, but seeing the radio-TV tower gives me an idea and I turn on the car radio and give the band a twirl. KGAS and KCOY are off the air which is strictly illegal but I catch something on KNES that isn't the before-dinner music it's supposed to be and I tune it in as best I can which isn't well because it's beamed in the other direction and just about blow another temper muscle, damn if the radio isn't talking about me.

". . . made his influence first felt with the unexpected construction of GASCOYNE CENTER in nineteen forty-nine. Yet now fifteen years later perhaps only as few as a hundred people in the city can be certain they have ever seen his face, and still fewer have spoken with him. Who is GASCOYNE? What does he look like? Where does he hide? Does he even exist? Many of us think we see him every day—a paper-thin old man driving an old car which in its day was just a little too flashy—but no one is ever certain. We will not have long to wait, however, it— One moment please. Excuse us ladies and gentlemen, Police Commissioner O'Mallollolly is here in the studio and would like to speak a few words."

"Thank you ladies and gentlemen. First I'd like to tell all you people out there how much we appreciate—" and then there's a sort of twittering zip sound and then complete silence and so it sounds to me like the whole thing was on tape and somebody took it off in a damn hurry, well at least nobody has to listen to O'Mallollolly's Gettysburg Address, though I'm beginning to wonder what is going on in that place.

Still heading down Ben Hur Boulevard I try to check

out the rearview but the lousy thing comes off in my hand and I have to hold it up like a pocket mirror, hardly worth the bother because I've seen the sight before which is six black and white Mercurys filled with state troopers and followed by the red Porsche. They've probably all got their safety belts fastened. They're that type, these troopers. Probably singing O'Mallollolly Uber Alles or inspecting each other's private parts.

I toss the mirror on the seat and begin to wonder if O'Mallollolly is making this fuss to get me to walk right into his hands with a big public arrest and all that with lots of pictures. A chance I've got to take, just can't sit around and watch the place go up in smoke.

I slow down a couple of blocks from GASCOYNE CENTER and from what I can see the place is surrounded by cop cars and God knows how many cops but I really have to laugh at the piddling crowd he's collected to watch the show. It's damn clear nobody gives a used fart what O'Mallollolly's doing and he's made a complete failure out of his attempt to capture the public imagination if it's got any.

But I'm getting too damn close so I pull the Kaiser into the GASCOYNE CENTER ANNEX TWO PARKING RAMP LOT and park the car in the space reserved for me in front of the alley fire exit and as I climb out damn if the six patrol cars don't come waddling in the place followed by the red tin can. "Charge 'em double," I shout to the attendant and duck down the basement stairwell.

Below I unlock my private tunnel door and step inside

and close it behind me and throw the three heavy bolts. It'll take a cannon to open that and I turn on the lights and make my way down the tunnel which is just a great big water-main pipe with yellow linoleum for a floorway and lights strung up above. I come to the GASCOYNE CENTER ANNEX ONE PARKING RAMP LOT tunnel junction and turn left and switch on the lights for the next section and switch them off for the one behind. Finally I come to the door in the basement of GASCOYNE CENTER and throw back the three bolts and open it and step into the basement. There's no one there. The basement unguarded might mean O'Mallollolly does want me here and knows how I get in and out, though I can't be sure. Can't be sure of anything anymore.

I trot over to the service elevator and push the button and watch the lights as the thing comes down from the sixth floor, BIG DADDY OFFICES. The door slides back and I climb in and push fourteen and up we go, though I'm not very happy about this ride since the floor is littered with papers from I can't tell what departments and a couple of beer bottles, nonreturnable wouldn't you know it, and the stinking contents of a couple of ashtrays, filthy habit, which all makes me pretty angry. The elevator stops and opens at fourteen, DOCUMENTS AND RECORDS for all my companies located outside GASCOYNE CENTER, and the place is the worst mess you've ever seen in your life. I step out and see that the incinerator next to the elevator is so crammed with papers that if anyone lit a match the whole building even though it's fireproof would go up with a bang, and it's damn hard for me to visualize the asshole who got the idea to fill the whole thing up at once like that, a bright-eyed college kid no doubt.

The rest of the place makes me want to close my eyes and count sheep but it's hardly the atmosphere for that. About two hundred filing cabinets are open and have been emptied onto the floor which is solid with papers and photographs and negatives and movie film and recording tape and over in the corner about twenty jokers are having a party. My employees. This sort of thing really makes an employer feel good.

I scramble through the mess over to File X which is a walk-in safe that hangs over the street in such a way it can't be broken into from the outside. It's been emptied but the contents are all outside the door spilling all over a large handcart with Municipal Police, A. O'Mallollolly, Police Commissioner, stenciled on it—and it's pretty clear they're intending to haul the stuff away as evidence and boy I hate to think what they'll do with it. There's not a damn thing I can do about it the way the incinerator's jammed up and I really doubt that any of my loyal employees would be willing to lift a finger at this particular moment. I'm damn tempted to light a match and run but the trouble is it's my barn too.

What can I do but turn away and get out of the place and so out the main door I go and up the staircase also jammed with papers and up to the fifteenth floor. Some yokel has pushed over and broken into the BIG DADDY

SUPER SWELL KOLA machine and the stuff is spilled all over the hallway, what a mess when mixed with paper.

I walk into Chester's office and the phone jacks of his little switchboard are all pulled out hanging limp and this creep is going through his desk.

"What the hell you think you're doing?" I ask.

"What does it look like?"

"Looting," I say.

"That's it."

When you come right down to it what does it matter and what can I do about it? I go out the other door into the secretarial bay and there's another creep who's stacking electric typewriters onto a handcart. My typewriters. He looks at me and says "Hi!" with a smile and keeps on stacking my typewriters. This is sort of exasperating but hell I can't go around the whole building all night saying Say fellow please don't steal my typewriters. Keep calm I tell myself and turn to go out and notice this fellow laid out on the floor and wonder what they ever did with Chester. Then I slip down the hall to the office I use when I come here which isn't very often, the last time was nine years ago as a matter of fact, and it looks like the place was hit by a grenade. The desk and chair and phone are all broken up in little pieces and the plate-glass window is all blown out and a pretty stiff breeze is coming through the hole. I stick my head out and look down and my don't they look just like black ants, and it looks like a few more battalions have arrived but I still have to laugh at the pisspoor crowd O'Mallollolly's whipped up, maybe

two hundred people in all minus a hundred who're probably plainclothesmen. If there's anything to make me feel
good at the moment, that's it. I can just see O'Mallollolly
chewing on his cigar and fingernails saying to Subcommissioner MacTule or somebody, "Christ you've got to fix
up my public image, they're not eating it up!" He doesn't
even know a damn thing about rigging elections, the slob,
and boy will he be sorry.

I pull my head back in and go up the stairway to the
roof and it looks like maybe good news time is starting up
again because there's my little Hughes chopper sitting
right there on the landing pad, Chester the dimwit forgot
to tell me they'd fixed it and brought it back, well so
there's a way out of this mess though I've never done
a takeoff or landing solo.

That cheers me up enough that I decide to go back
down and see what else can be salvaged and I slip down
the stairs through my office and go back into Chester's to
see if he left any handy phone lists around. The looting
creep's gone and I start shuffling through the papers in
Chester's desk but the trouble is I'm pretty badly far-
sighted and left my glasses somewhere and anyway it's
been so long since I've read anything but signs and things
like that that I've pretty well forgotten how to read,
haven't even looked at the *Herald* or *Times* for thirty
years, but that's the sort of thing I pay all these people for.

I give up that idea and walk into the secretarial bay
and wonder about that Negro laid out there and think
maybe he's one of O'Mallollolly's crew. About then some

character charges around the corner with a handcart and about bowls me over and pushes it over to some electric adding machines and starts loading them up, pretty disgusting, though I must say the guy's got guts and an enterprising spirit, we all start out that way. He sees me watching him and he looks up and says, "You work here?"

"No," I say thinking it best to keep my identity secret under these conditions, "I'm just a friend of Chester's."

"Yeah, too bad about him," he says pointing to the stiff.

"Who's that?" I ask.

"Who's that? I thought you said you were a friend."

"That's not Chester," I say.

He looks at me a minute and says, "We got the right Chester, don't we? I'm talking about Chester Jones," and he points a pretty firm finger at that colored corpse.

Well it hits me with both barrels then and really burns me right up, Chester colored all these years and nobody ever told me, boy what kind of friends do I have? Worst piece of news I've had in years. Turns out I've been depending on a goddamn Negro. Explains a lot and a hell of a lot, just when I've been about to blame myself for all this mess. And nobody ever told me, that's what really pisses me off, really does. Well I get the point loud and clear and as soon as I get things back running right the first thing I'm going to do is find my glasses and go through every lousy employee photograph and fire the whole lot of them, just can't depend on them.

*

I head out of there as fast as I can go because that's one thing I want to forget about quick, and slip down to floor thirteen where I run into about twenty cops in the hallway loitering around and getting ready to rape the secretaries who seem to be looking forward to it like the one in the corner who's getting an intimate talking to by some cop while another cop's waving her brassiere around. A bunch of state troopers are playing games with their rifles and prying up squares of plastic tile spelling out nasty words in the floor and one pervert is throwing staplers at the light fixtures and making a big mess everywhere. When I walk through they all sort of stop and stare a moment and then go back to what they're doing which is destroying all my property, every last piece of it.

I walk down the hall and look in on a couple of the radio-TV studios but the joint's such a screaming mess jammed with my employees and cops all soaked up in liquor that if they let the city zoo loose here the place'd seem like a tea party by comparison, and all I hope is that all this sin is being broadcast all over the city.

I'm about to take the elevator down to the twelfth floor but the damn thing is filled with secretaries and clerks having a party and slopping liquor everywhere and singing like cats in heat and you can imagine what else. I hit the stairs instead and squeeze through about five discussion groups and a couple of bridge parties and poker parties and what looks like is shaping up as a gangbang, and it's pretty damn clear to me that if you don't keep

225

people working like dogs they'll behave like rabbits and monkeys. You've got to put them inside little boxes with their work and throw away the key for eight hours every day and then chase them out of the box as soon as you can after their time is up, give them fringe benefits like pastel toilet paper and maybe a Christmas party to make them feel grateful but otherwise if you give them an inch they'll take a mile like this and start breaking up the place and develop loose morals.

The *Herald-Times* editorial offices on floor thirteen are a shambles like somebody's about to start a bonfire and everything there's out of hand so I catch a service elevator finally and speed her down to the second floor where the auditorium is because if anybody's in charge here it'll be there and I can present the bastard with a few questions, namely on what the hell he thinks he's doing on and with my premises.

This is going to be a little tricky because what I've got hanging around GASCOYNE CENTER and a lot of other places is a picture of an ivy league type around thirty and blond with a toothpaste-ad smile and everybody thinks it's me GASCOYNE. Of course that's what I want because I figure people work better if they think they're working for some young but not too young up-and-coming fellow. Makes them think the whole shebang is nice and good-humored and if it isn't it's because, so they're supposed to think, there's somebody balling up the works between them and the toothpaste kid and nothing to get really excited about because the young knight on the white steed

will come dashing to the rescue some day with a pat on the
back and a three percent raise. To me the toothpaste kid
looks like a real shit, but the public relations people said
that's all right and not to worry because it's all right if he
looks like a real shit to some people some of the time or
even all of the time because they say to themselves How
can I be happy working for an ass like that and they keep
on being unhappy, but boy do they keep on working too.
You've got to play the angles. But no I wouldn't have my
picture up here on the walls of hundreds of offices, for one
thing it's against my policy and another is that I'm not
very photogenic. I don't know anybody of my age that is,
I'm no spring chicken anymore, but what counts is not my
face but my name which is a lot easier to carry around
than a wad of cash and like in the old days when anybody
just dropped the name of the King of England everybody'd throw themselves down on their knees. Well I
want it that when they hear the name GASCOYNE they
reach straight for their wallets, don't give a damn whether
they smile or not.

I pop out of the elevator and shove my way through a
bunch of cops standing around some cases of beer making
slurping noises and squeeze through the door of the
CELESTE GASCOYNE MATERNAL MEMORIAL AUDITORIUM
and find the place sardine-packed with cops and former
employees of mine drinking beer and stuff out of paper
cups and all jabbering away like they were being paid for
it.

Up on the stage this pervert is blowing into the microphone and yelling "Testing, one-two-three, can you hear me out there?" And on the stage curtain above him somebody has pinned a couple of paper letters of a slogan or something and hasn't gotten around to finishing it. I slip back out the door and around the hallway to the side stage entrance and go in that and come out on the stage where I stop and give a significant pause at the audience. A couple of nice people notice my presence and then I walk over to this type who's spreading his germs all over the microphone and say, "All right junior beat it. I've got a few words to say."

"Who the hell do you think you are?" he asks.

"It's me, GASCOYNE," I say in such a way the microphone picks it up and broadcasts it all over the auditorium. Things suddenly go quiet down below and people turn around and look up.

"Prove it," says junior.

I whip out my driver's license before he can come out with some wisecrack I'm sure he's got buzzing around in his pea-brained pinhead. He looks at it and then at me and gives it back and looks at me a second and says, "Okay," and walks off the stage waving to some broad with a tight blouse down below.

First of all I clear my throat to let them all know I have a few words to say.

"Ladies and gentlemen," I say, "excuse me for getting up here like this on the stage of the CELESTE GASCOYNE MATERNAL MEMORIAL AUDITORIUM named after my dear mother who died fifty years ago giving her life to the very city we happen to have the honor of living in right this very moment, and it is an honor. That as a matter of fact is what I want to talk to you about tonight."

Maybe I shouldn't have said that because about then somebody shakes up a beer bottle and shoots it at the ceiling which gets a lot of people pretty damp and makes them noisy, but I decide to go on anyway.

"As you know our city is being screwed up at the moment by somebody who shouldn't be allowed to go on with it and you know I'm talking about none other than Police Commissioner O'Mallollolly."

Well at the mention of his name I expect to get some sort of rise and am ready to put up with it but there's not a damned sound besides the general racket down there that's getting worse and worse. As a public speaker I know damn well I'm not a Jesus Christ but I know also I've heard worse so I figure the problem is that these people have all gone and stupefied their minds with liquor and not in a few cases with sex. This pretty well leaves me flapping my flippers high and dry but I can't stop there.

"Now if this O'Mallollolly is not stopped dead in his tracks, folks, hey folks, you'll find pretty soon that if you just only want to take even a drink or go to bed with your wife you'll have to ask him permission or pay a tax."

That catches a few but not very many. Sometimes you wonder what they do want.

"Now folks I hate to bring this up really but I'm afraid the way you're behaving here now is almost irresponsible and careless and it's undermining the free enterprise sys-

tem which has made our city what it is. Now let's all turn
over a new leaf and quietly leave the building those of
you who are not on the evening shift, and those of you
who are would you please get back to your offices and
let's put out an edition of the *Herald* which'll save democ-
racy for our children and other future generations."

About this point I don't think anybody can hear a damn
thing because everybody's blabbing to his neighbor like
it's the last chance they'll ever have. And then there's
some tables at the side with beer cases on them and for
some reason underneath them's become a popular place
to be and all you can see is a jumble of uniforms and
ladies' garments. Well I don't know what I'm doing up on
the stage frankly except the view's better, but that's not
what I want at the moment so I sort of amble off to the
stage door and am rather pissed off that not one person
seems to notice that I'm leaving, me who's been paying
their salaries all these years.

Out in the hall there are more policemen than ever and
drinking, all of them, like fish and not a few pissing
against the walls. Pretty hard to keep my temper about
that one but what can I do? Might as well get out of here
while the getting's still good so I catch the service elevator and push the fifteen button and up she goes. Almost
tempted to stop by the Urban-Suburban Water and
Telephone Company offices but what's the use now and
I pass that up and get out on fifteen. The floor's still
pretty quiet and I hop through my office and up the stairs

to the roof and flick on the heliport landing lights and pack myself into the chopper bubble. I start her up and she turns over nicely and smooths out, gauges okay, and I wait a minute for the temperature to rise to Operating.

This gives me a moment to think and what really gets me is not having to pull out of GASCOYNE CENTER because after all whatever they do I still own the damn thing, but why they're letting me run around like this with nobody chasing me and nobody really giving a damn about anything. I'd be a damn fool if I didn't say, Okay O'Mallollolly you've won this round, but the idiot doesn't seem to know it or how to take advantage of it and it's pretty clear he's messing things up so badly he couldn't get elected as City Birdbath Superintendent. Maybe nobody's in charge here, but that'd be just too good to be true and it doesn't figure at all. But something's the matter somewhere and I'd sure like to know where.

The temp's up to Operating and I try to remember how to wiggle the controls to get off the ground, seemed easy when I did it last with the guy teaching me how to fly. First I rev up the motor and change the pitch slightly and I can feel her wanting to lift and that seems right so I fool around with the rear rotor control and rock her back and forth a little. Finally I pull back on the throttle and pitch and the rotor chops into the air with a good solid *whomp-whomp* and up we go, straight up. I get about fifty feet up and hold it so I can straighten out a funny tilt I've got in the nose and also a sideways leaning that's pretty uncomfortable and bad for the balance. I fool around with the rear rotor some more and get the tilt fixed but too far and now the tail droops and the damn thing's going backwards and for some idiot reason instead of undoing what I just did I play around with the main throttle and pitch and the thing just goes backwards faster straight into what I just remember is there which is the radio-TV tower. I hear a *bang-bang* and a *zzzz* noise and then a crunching and crashing and screaming and then *twang-twang* as the main rotor gets into the act. Suddenly the whole thing flips over on its back and there's this horrible crashing and thumping and the nose falls and the thing comes to a sudden stop, nose down with a wrenching metal noise and it's dead quiet except for the wind whistling through the holes in the plastic bubble.

This is a fine kettle of fish to be in but all I can do is push open the side cockpit door and look down and it seems we've somehow got attached to the tower about seventy feet up, very firmly I hope but damned if I'm going to sit inside with a stopwatch to see how long the thing holds.

I reach outside and grab some rungs or struts or something, I can't tell because the light's not too good, and start to pull myself out of the machine. About this point something gives a lurch and I'm forced to choose right now between the tower and the chopper and of course choose the tower but can't seem to pull myself out and then there's another lurch and so I say hell with the tower and pull myself back into the cockpit and decide to wait

232

until the thing settles down, fastening my seat belt just in case.

Good thing I do because without the slightest warning the thing begins to fall like somebody just let go. I clasp my hands together and try to think of something besides flying and then there's this big *clang* and everything's dead quiet and I can hardly believe it but the thing's landed square on its feet. I unfasten my seat belt and pull myself up out of the seat which has collapsed to the floor and push myself out of the bubble and take a look at the wreck, and that's about all it can be called anymore. Another twenty-five grand down the drain, as they say, damn expensive day this one. But besides having a sore ass I'm all right which is the thing that counts.

I limp over to the stairs and down to the service elevator and hop in that and get her down to the basement as fast as she'll go and then I duck into the tunnel locking it behind where it occurs to me what with my pocketful of Ritz crackers I could stay down here a hell of a long time, but the trouble is that'd be a little boring and I think what I really need is to get out of town and take a little vacation.

I pop out of there then as fast as my sore ass permits and find things looking up in the ANNEX TWO LOT because the Kaiser's still there apparently unharmed and the cop cars and Porsche are all gone, strange indeed. I climb in the Kaiser and boy does it hurt to sit down, and I fire her

Gascoyne

up and scoot out the fire exit and barrel down the alley
and swing back onto Ben Hur Boulevard and head for the
hills. It's almost dark now and the rush hour traffic's just
about off the streets and everybody going home to wonder why there's no TV tonight.

I slip her in the fast lane and run her up to sixty and
hope some damn fool won't decide to make a left turn in
front of me. About now I figure O'Mallollolly's got himself
into some deep trouble and maybe somebody else's taken
over Police Tower but I won't know about that until I
find somebody to replace that sneak Chester and next
time I'm going to have things a little more decentralized.
For my vacation what I ought to do is go north to the
capital and brief one of the boys there and send him
down here to take over and straighten things out and get
them ready for when I can come back and run things like
they were. Just then Marge calls so I know at least the
phone company hasn't cut off my private long-distance
circuit, things aren't so bad after all.

"Hi Marge what's new?"

"Well dear I'm up in Condor's Crag now and I don't
like the looks of the place."

"Are you alone?" I ask.

"Well yes I hope so," she says. "I left Tom Rasper down
in the bar."

I'm glad about that and I'm glad she's talking again.

"There's something creepy about this place," she says,
"and you know, somebody's living here now."

"You're kidding. How do you know?"

234

"Well there's all sorts of stuff in the icebox and the bed's been slept in and there's an electric razor in the bath and this morning's *Times* right here in the main living room and there are hot coals in the fireplace."

"Hmm. Yes it does look like somebody's living there doesn't it?"

"Well what do I do dear if he comes in?"

"Make up a story, that's all Marge."

"Well what really bothers me is I have the feeling he's around here watching me now. You know how thick the forest is right up to the house and how the wind blows all the time, it's impossible to be sure you're alone. Well really dear I've seen the place and it's in very good condition and now I think I really ought to get back down to the main road before it gets too dark."

"Okay Marge."

Then she sort of gasps.

"What's the matter Marge?"

"The closet door's opening!" she whispers.

"Just a mouse probably," I say.

"No! Ah!" she says.

"What?"

"A body!"

"What?"

"A body just fell out of the closet!"

"Well don't just stand there, go see whose it is," I say.

The receiver goes *clankety-clank* and I turn on the air horn and blast through a red light and miss just by inches the whole goddamn fire department. I pick up the rearview and see they're going the other way down Ben Hur toward downtown and I stick my head out the window and about drive in to the curb when I see smoke and flames roaring out of the top of GASCOYNE CENTER like a Roman candle, but no sweat since the thing's insured. I hear receiver noises and Marge's back on again.

"Good God," she says, "it's O'Mallollolly!"

"What?"

"Yes! Dead!"

"How?"

"I couldn't tell."

"Hmm," I say and that one doesn't seem to make any sense at all and then I remember the last time I saw him was in the battle for Police Tower almost eight hours ago and when I heard him on the radio his voice was recorded, so there was time for him to go up to Condor's Crag or be carried up there, well that takes care of him.

"Dear I've simply got to get out of here, I don't like this at all."

"Of course Marge, but first could you look around for a few clues?"

"Ohmygod!"

"What now?" I ask.

"I'm looking out the big picture window and the sun's just going down way up here and there's something like a horrible creature standing by the telephone pole, how ghastly it is! What should I do?"

"Keep calm and don't move. Tell me what it looks like Marge."

236

"Well in this light it looks sort of greenish grayish about the height of a man and it's standing on its hind legs actually quite erect. It's got long black curved claws."

Of course, it's the giant tree sloth I think.

"And," she goes on, "the thing is holding a pair of wire cutters in its claws."

"Don't worry Marge it's only some Harvard man dressed up as a giant tree sloth."

"That's what I'm afraid of dear. I think I'm going to scream."

"Don't do anything rash Marge, keep calm."

"It's climbing the telephone pole! It left its claws behind."

"Well don't worry Marge a man dressed up like a giant tree sloth probably feels like acting like one now and then."

"He's near the top of the pole now, near the wires. Dear I think he's going to cut the wires. Ohmygod!"

"What?"

"There's a man crouching about thirty feet away with a high-powered rifle with a telescope on it pointed right at the thing on the pole!"

"Yes, yes?"

"The creature's reaching for the wires. No, he's put the cutters into one hand and with the other he's taking off his head."

"Oh?"

"There it comes," she says. "Ohmygod! It can't be! It's Rufus Roughah!"

Well I guess the bastard did cut the wires after all because that's the last I hear of old Marge, nothing to worry about since she's pretty resourceful and should be able to take care of this one like she's done the rest. But what pisses me off is that I've gone and spent all that money sending her up there, hotel bills and expensive meals, and then it turns out that Roughah's alive and so the place isn't up for sale. But wait a minute, supposing he does get bumped off by the guy with the rifle? Everything'll be back where it was and the place will be for sale, okay.

Then suddenly things go wham-bang and fit together and I see what's been going on for the last couple of days and why O'Mallollolly was at the Mirindaranda Road Roughah place the afternoon of the murder which I see now was a phony put-up job meant to throw me off the real scent which boils down to O'Mallollolly and Roughah getting together secretly using Nancy and Nadine but probably not Dmitri to get me out of the way and fix my wagon by taking over all of Police Tower and City Hall and subverting my own employees at GASCOYNE CENTER and generally messing up the works to get me out of the picture. But something went wrong and O'Mallollolly got kidnapped and bumped off and now probably Roughah too which still leaves me and somebody else I don't know anything else about.

But I still think it's a good idea to get out of town for awhile and am about to stop for gas at the Ben Húr Boulevard BIG DADDY SERV-UR-SELPH but damn if all the lights aren't off and the thing closed up, supposed to be open twenty-four hours a day just like me, so I turn right onto Vieworama Ridge Road and head up over the hill and hold up the rearview and find there's nobody following. The Kaiser seems to be running real smooth now but all of a sudden near the crest of the hill the temp needle flies over to Boil and I wonder what now. Still I hit the crest all right and start down the other side and expect to see the thing cool off some but it doesn't so I turn off the motor and coast down to the bright lights of the Mirindaranda strip and turn it back on just before I hit Mirindaranda Road and she catches and is still running, good old buggy.

I catch the Mirindaranda Road signal green and bounce the dip and turn left with the tires squealing and just as I get the thing straightened out six black unmarked Ford sedans shoot out of a side street and I hold up the rearview to take a better gander and see first the little blue Porsche coming next and after that the little red one and last of all a long black limousine which I can't tell the make of at that distance.

This sort of rattles me and I decide to give them a run for their money and hit the supercharger and run her up to fifty-five which is the fastest you can go on Mirindaranda until you get caught by the signals, but hell with them. Then all of a sudden the old engine starts running really rough and though I can't see it I know there's steam coming out of the front because something's beginning to smell bad, must be out of water dammit, and there's nothing to do but stop at the BIG DADDY STATION coming up so

Gascoyne

I scoot over to the right lane and the motor starts
knocking and clanging and I hate to think what's going on
inside. It gets worse and something starts screaming and
howling like the devil inside, sounds like a rod, so I switch
off the ignition and let her coast, only two hundred yards
to go. Just then the phone rings and I wonder who the
hell it can be.

"Hello," I say.

"Hello," says a woman's voice I don't recognize, "is this
Bernie?"

"Hell no, it's me GASCOYNE."

"Who?"

"GASCOYNE!"

"Oh," she says. "Well you must work with Bernie
then—"

I say no but the gasbag doesn't hear me.

"—and I wonder if you could come over and fix my
television set because I don't seem to be able to get anything on it on any station and I have to stay home tonight
because Charles—"

Well I hang up on that one just as I roll up to the BIG
DADDY STATION and bounce over the curb and stop her in
front of the gas pumps and climb out. Well it's real smoke
pouring out of the hood cracks now and I lean back in to
pull the hood latch handle and the damn thing comes off
in my hand and the hood stays closed and the paint's
turning black with bubbles and blisters. A couple of at-
tendants run up and turn a hose on the thing but it just
makes a lot of steam on top and doesn't get inside at all.

Then these unmarked Ford sedans start arriving from all directions, must be about fifty of them, some pulling into the station and others stopping in the streets and cops start piling out in uniforms I've never seen before. In a second the two Porsches pull up and next this limousine but I can't see who's in it because it's got shades in the back and they're all down and what really gets me is I've never seen that kind of car before and don't have any idea of what it is and it just sits there and nobody gets out. Looks damned expensive.

I stand there watching the show and wonder what the hell is going on and a bunch of cops get behind the Kaiser and push it into the center of Mirindaranda Road where it finally bursts into flames and lights up the whole place like a Boy Scout jamboree. Then they come back heading toward me who's just standing there minding my own business and nibbling on a Ritz cracker and they all surround me, hundreds of them there are, and one of them yells, "Don't kick him in the balls because he hasn't got any," which is sure as hell not true but it does save me a lot of pain I will say.

That's about all I know right now and I'm not one to cry over spilt milk though it does sort of rub me the wrong way that the fire department didn't bother to put out the fire in GASCOYNE CENTER. Everybody's suing me and my assets are either all tied up or going to pot and I could use a little cash, you know how lawyers are about twiddling their thumbs until they're dead sure there are

241

cookies in the cookie jar. But anyway, when you come right down to it I haven't got much to complain about since I was smart enough to salt a little away here and there, namely in Powderville which is about a hundred and fifty miles out of town right smack in the desert, so in the meantime I've got just enough to squeak by on.

So I'm just being nice and quiet until the time comes I can go back into town and give a piece of my mind to my so-called friends and I just sent my man George off on the Greyhound bus to town to take a little look-see at the scenery there, he's the one who went back in last week and rescued the '52 Hudson convertible I've got now and also my house trailer, and I told him to find out just one thing and that's who's running the shooting match now because I can't make any big plans until I know that little item, and next week I'll send him up north to the capital to see what's going on, haven't heard a peep out of anybody up there.

But I've been pretty busy since I got here though Powderville's no great shakes of a town, a bunch of chicken farms and junkyards. It's the first burg out of town where people start having car trouble and running out of money at the same time, you know how the desert is, but there's a lot of opportunity out here and this is one I'm not letting slip by. I've already got options on all the land the big interstate freeway's supposed to cross thanks to a little deal I pulled with the town council, bunch of drunks though they may be, and I just finished working my way into part ownership of the Savage Desert Reptile Farm

—THE WORLD'S LARGEST!, which isn't true, but it's going to be a lot bigger as soon as I scrape up the cash to get seven alligators out of hock in the train depot, bastards must have fed them top sirloin all the way from Pensacola, Florida. But those alligators and me are going to put Powderville on the map some day soon and there's no sense sitting around and letting somebody else do it, so right now I'm heading out the main highway east with a bunch of SAVAGE DESERT REPTILE FARM signs in the trunk of the old Hudson to plant in the landscape to catch the suckers coming from back east who'll pay anything for a cold beer while the kiddies watch the snakes and lizards.

I still get a lot of driving in out here, it's the best way to keep cool, though the Hudson starts knocking and getting hot under the floorboards over forty-five, and right now I'm running past the DESERT JEWEL BEAUTIFUL ESTATES TRACT which has got the streets all laid out and a few fake phone poles on this dry lake bed but no houses because we haven't found anybody yet with the proper frontier spirit to put down a thousand bucks to get the boom rolling. Rome wasn't built in a day and it sure wasn't built by people who asked silly questions about electricity and water and sewers first. I think this country's getting too damn soft.

About now the phone rings but I wait and it turns out to be two shorts and a long which is for the quack who calls himself a doctor out here and not for me which probably means that some cactus farmer fell off his tractor. I don't get much in the way of phone calls these days but seeing as I kind of need the rest that's all right, the heat out here's pretty exhausting and right now that old sun is zeroing in on the rearview and so I flip it down just as a Greyhound bus goes screaming past me about thirty miles over the speed limit, but from now on it's going to be a little cooler so it won't be so bad planting the signs, about five of them I've got to do this evening.

The site of my next Big Daddy Station comes into view on the left, nothing there now but a pile of rocks and some stakes and a few colored flags but as soon as we get this one up and the one planned for the other end of Powderville it'll teach those Powderville yokels that if they won't let me join them I'll beat them at their own game. Just beyond here I think will be a good place for the next sign so I cross over the left lane and roll her into the sagebrush and hop out and untie the trunk lid and pull out a big one, See The SERPENT That Bit Eve!!, and hammer it into the ground. Well that looks pretty good so I hop back inside and take a swig from the old canteen, having worked up a sweat over that one even though the sun's going down. Then I drop her in low and plow through the sagebrush for a couple of hundred yards and stop and put up the next one, See CLEOPATRA'S ASP!!!, which is about enough for this neck of the woods so I roll her back through the beer cans onto the highway and head on east. I figure that in two more months we'll have so many signs on the highway coming from the East that you'll be able to drive for three hundred miles without ever being completely out of sight of one, no better place than the desert to do a little brainwashing.

I run her up to about forty and let a couple of semis pass and settle back in the seat and hold her on that long white line, thinking that what I really ought to do is pull back over to the side and take a little snooze until the heat goes down some more, and so that's just what I do. I shut off the motor but since the Hudson's seat won't go back, probably some chewing gum in the works, I stretch out sideways and prop my head against the door and watch the cars go by, wondering which ones are going to have the good sense to stop at the SAVAGE DESERT REPTILE FARM and plunk down a buck-fifty a head, every little bit helps. . . .